Best Wi

Meetings & Partings

By

R J Turner

Published by Leaf by Leaf Press 2025
www.leafbyleafpress.com

ISBN 978-1-0686890-0-0

Cover photo
De Luan / Alamy Stock Photo
Chronicle / Alamy Stock Photo

Dedication.

My daughters, Martha and Bryher, my Granddaughters, Hollie, Kari and Bethany and my great Granddaughters. Libby and April.

Acknowledgements

I would like to thank the members of Leaf by Leaf Press for their support and to John Heap in particular for turning my draft copy into a publishable product. I would also like to thank my son, Robert, for the cover design.

Meetings & Partings

By

R J Turner

Huw's Story

Chapter One

'It's not for the love of gold I go, and it's not for the love of fame,
But fortune might smile on me, and I might win a name.'
From '*The Shores of Americay*' an Irish Immigration song.

'Good morning, Mr Morris, and how are ye today?'

That's the Captain speaking as he passes me on his daily tour of inspection. Captain Thomas Evans is a Welshman like myself, but from Swansea in the south. He is short and stout, with a round, ruddy face, a white cloud of hair and a curly beard. In fact, give him a cutlass and he could be a pirate. He roared when I told him that. We have become well acquainted as this fine ship has made its way across the Atlantic in a mere fourteen days. Now here we are crossing the Irish Sea on the last lap and making our way towards Liverpool. Yes, I can already see a smudge on the horizon that will form into those mountains where I spent my younger days slaving- yes, it was almost slavery – in the slate quarries between Dolgellau and Machynlleth. Mind, that was almost twenty years ago, thousands of miles since. Now Huw Morris is returning as a rich man.

It has been a splendid crossing. The Atlantic storms seem to have taken a year off. The Lady of Shallot is not the newest, largest, fastest or most luxurious of ships, but she is reliable and clean and the crew are friendly and efficient. The Captain had introduced himself almost as soon as the voyage began. He had probably heard of my wealth, but he did not treat me as a special case. After all he had carried many a rich man across the ocean in his time. He understood that I had chosen his ship because he did not go in for special treatment or social gatherings. He was interested in my life and I was interested in his, so we spent many an evening swapping stories.

Even so, I could not avoid comparing this crossing with my journey to New York all those years ago. The days of the coffin ships were over, and even in steerage conditions had improved somewhat, but as a poor emigrant on a small, ancient steamer, my passage paid by a friend, I was treated like any other emigrant; that is as less than human. And the weather was appalling. We travelled through terrible storms most of the way, the small ship bucking in the huge waves, so that we were confined to the lower deck where even the healthiest were constantly sea-sick and contagious diseases spread rapidly in the fetid air and inadequate, sanitary arrangements. It took us more than four weeks to batter our way across the Atlantic; four weeks of near hell.

But it was not just the conditions of the journey that made it so unpleasant. It was also my state of mind. I was angry and very bitter about the way I had been treated, and I hated almost everyone. I had very little hope that things would be better for me in that new land. You see, I had been found guilty of causing criminal damage – in fact blowing up a tunnel built to carry the water from the new reservoir called Lake Vyrnwy to Liverpool – when I had nothing to do with that pointless vandalism and had tried to dissuade those foolish fellow countrymen actually involved to give it up.

The one person who could have proved me innocent – the girl I was with at the time – did not appear in court and did not try to visit me at all. I thought she had loved me and indeed we had actually made love while trapped together in that damned tower on the edge of the lake. But when I tried to make contact with her she seemed to have disappeared off the face of the earth. So I was sent to prison for seven years.

Strangely it was the man who had been my rival for the affections of that young girl, who began to investigate this miscarriage of justice and eventually after much hard work had my conviction quashed. Philip Lever had changed so much in such a short time. When I first met him in the valley, where my father and I were demolishing the old village of Llanwddyn before the lake began to fill, he was an arrogant, self- centred medical student and a bit of a dilettante. (Oh yes, I can use words like that these days, thanks to Julia) We both fell for John Noble's beautiful stepdaughter, Amy, but it was my affections she returned. He told me that when he first learned of my arrest and imprisonment he was glad, especially as it cleared the way for him to pursue Amy, but that proved impossible as her stepfather would not allow any contact with her.

But Philip soon began to feel guilty about what had happened to me and decided to visit my home, where he had briefly been a guest, to see how they were faring without me and he was shocked to discover that my father had been killed in an accident and that my sister, Nan, had disappeared.

To try to find out more he had visited the quarry where my father and I used to work and by a strange twist of fate he became its medical officer. It was then that his views began to change. He could not believe the conditions under which the workers toiled, the dangers they faced for less than a proper living wage. He soon discovered that the quarry owners were ruthless employers, whose only concern was profit.

It was while he shared the lives of these quarry men (He even began to learn Welsh) that he discovered the injustice of my imprisonment and eventually secured my release. I was very grateful indeed, but soon discovered that my problems had not ended when the prison doors closed behind me. The quarry where I had been a skilled worker would not reemploy me and I soon discovered that I had been blacklisted by all the other quarry owners. Again, it was Philip who helped me, suggesting that I make a new life for myself in America and by paying for my passage.

The first thing I intend to do when I land in Liverpool is to find Philip Lever, to shake his hand and repay my debt.

During these ruminations I have been leaning on the rail watching the bow wave go by. Now a change in the engine noise has made me look up to see that we have moved much closer to land. There are my mountains, rising from the morning mist. I love them and loathe them at the same time.

An officer strides across the deck towards me.

'Captain's complements, Mr Morris. I am to inform you that we will be in the Mersey quite soon and that you should make arrangements for disembarking.'

With that he strides away. I look up towards the bridge and salute the captain who smiles and nods in return. Then I make my way to my cabin.

I have no idea yet where I will stay in Liverpool or where my plans may lead me so I have not brought much luggage, after all what I haven't got I can simply buy when I need it. My cases, except one small overnight bag have already been packed and taken to the luggage compartment to be unloaded onto the quay and the clothes I shall wear when I leave the ship have been laid out neatly on the bed. I aim not to look too much like an American, or a particularly rich man, so my dark grey suit is modest, though handmade, and my coat is black with an astrakhan collar, matching my hat.

When I am dressed, I push the clothes I have removed into the small bag –not very neatly I'm afraid, being used to someone else doing that for me these days. I check my wallet and documents, then glance in the full-length mirror set in the walnut wardrobe door, and am generally pleased with what I see. They say clothes maketh the man and there is some truth in that, but I have not allowed my body to turn to fat now that I no longer have to work physically to earn my crust. So here I am, Huw Morris, thirty-eight years old, not tall but well built, my dark curls now touched with grey and a neatly trimmed moustache hiding my full upper lip. There is the beginning of a slight pouch under each dark eye- after all I am no longer in the first flush of youth- but there is no loose flesh about the jowls.

I hear a loud blast from the ship's horn, pick up my bag and make my way back to the deck. Suddenly my self-confidence oozes away. We are stationary on the grey Mersey under an equally grey sky, awaiting the tugs to take us to our berth, and there in front of me is the same grey city I left all those years ago, and where I spent the unhappiest years of my life incarcerated in that dreadful jail.

I cannot not help but smile as I book in at the Adelphi. With immense care and courtesy, I was offered one of the best rooms, but turned it down as too large for my purpose and was shown to a pleasant room on the third floor. What caused my smile was the thought that if I had entered that sumptuous reception area in my previous existence I would undoubtedly been dragged out by a burly doorman and thrown onto the pavement, or sidewalk as I have been used to calling it.

Through the window of my room, I saw that the sun had come out so I decided to take a walk and get used to terra-firma again. With the parting of those grey clouds my jaundiced view of Liverpool faded somewhat and now I saw what a prosperous city it had become. I spent a while enjoying the magnificent cluster of buildings near St. George's Hall, built in the style of a much earlier era – Greek I think or Roman – Philip would know, when I found him, then I walked on through the more crowded, business-like streets, where loaded wagons pulled by sturdy horses and horse drawn cabs fought for space with motor vehicles, trams and intrepid pedestrians. Sometimes the whole panoply came to a cacophonous halt. I passed through a busy market and moved on towards the waterfront. Just before I reached the Mersey I passed under part of the overhead electric railway, which reminded me of the El in New York. The main difference between that city and this is the height of the buildings. The limited space in New York has been utilized by building upwards – everywhere there are these tall buildings turning the streets into canyons between cliffs of masonry but here in Liverpool land does not seem to be at a premium so the buildings are mostly good solid structures, just a few storeys high.

When I reached the river, I discovered that several large, handsome buildings had been erected in my absence. In fact, one of these was obviously just completed and a sign explained that it had something to do with the Port Authorities. But I was already tired of all this capitalistic opulence and wanted to see how those meaner streets behind the docks had fared since I rented a filthy little room there while I waited with so many other emigrants to board the ship for America.

As soon as I stepped into this less savoury district, which seemed almost unchanged, I was aware that I would be regarded as a 'toff' in this neighbourhood and needed to remain alert, but my attention was almost immediately grabbed by a torn poster on a high, smoke blackened wall. Surely I knew that face. A few yards on, was another poster, this time intact, and below the face, which someone had defaced with a large moustache, was the message, 'Mr Philip Lever, your Independent Candidate for such and such ward will be speaking tonight at St Alban's Church Hall, 7.30pm.' I stood gazing at the poster and wondering whether tonight was really this coming night and if so rejoicing at the ease with which I had found my old friend. We had completely lost touch during my American adventures but it was possible that our reunion would come very soon.

While I had been studying the poster a couple of suspicious looking characters had moved across to me. One man was taller than the other but both were thin and pale. I guessed they were what in America would have been called hoboes- I had in fact been one myself for a while-, in ill-fitting un-matched jackets and trousers and well-worn boots. The taller one came towards me and whispered, 'Got a few shilling to spare for a couple of blokes down on their luck, mate?'

Both men moved closer and I knew that my contributions would not be voluntary, but these were poor physical specimens and I had kept up my exercises when the hard work which had given strength to my muscles had ceased. In fact, I paid frequent visits to a well-known New York gymnasium where an evil looking guy called Buster Gut put me through my paces. Now I took a half sovereign from my coat pocket and held it out to the closest man.

'That should be enough to feed you both and get you thoroughly drunk for a while. Now I have to be on my way.'

The hand grabbed the sovereign and my wrist with it and I smelled his disgusting breath as he leaned in towards me. But instead of trying to pull my wrist away, as he expected, I did the opposite and pushed his arm into his gut with considerable force and when he doubled up and released his grip on my arm I gave him a shove backwards onto the pavement. He sat there confused with the sovereign spinning beside him. I turned to deal with the other guy but he had already disappeared.

As I strode away the man on the pavement muttered some obscenities, before grabbing the coin and shuffling off. I decided that I had seen enough of the seedy side of Liverpool and made my back to the main streets to look for somewhere to eat. On the way I found a pawnbroker and bought a coat, a suit that more or less fitted, and a pair of boots in my size. The clothes were clean but shabby, probably some skilled labourer's Sunday best, but they would look less conspicuous when I went to the meeting at St Alban's Hall.

It was raining as the cab dropped me a few streets away and when I reached the hall, I was surprised to find that it was crowded. Well, I thought, Philip seems to have plenty of support. I recognised him as soon as he walked onto the stage, but was disconcerted by the low growl from one section of the audience. Time had not been kind to Philip. He was still tall and slim, thin I would say, and rather stooped. His fair hair had receded so that his forehead seemed larger and was quite lined. But the most noticeable feature was his mouth which drooped beneath a pale moustache and made him look kinda sad.

A portly man in a check suit rose, cleared his throat, and waited for the audience to settle. When he introduced Philip there were more boos from that hostile group. The portly man sat down again and leant back in his chair which groaned as if it were about to collapse.

Philip stood up to polite applause and more boos from the expected quarter. I noticed that his voice was softer than in the old days but his enunciation was good so that he could easily be heard.

'Friends...'

'You aint no friend of mine, mate.'

This was followed by laughter.

'Friends...' Philip repeated more forcefully. I remembered that play Julia had taken me to see in New York. Shakespeare. Julius Caesar. Mark Anthony's ironic speech beginning 'Friends, Romans, countrymen...' But that was not how Philip continued.

'My friends, we are living through a period of change...'

'Yea, about two shilling and fourpence 'a'p'ny'

More laughter.

'A time when things have at last begun to improve for the working man...'

'Bet you aint done a proper day's work in your whole life.'

Raucous louder laughter.

There were shouts from the rest of the audience that the hecklers be quiet and to let them hear what Philip was saying. I looked across and saw the reason for the increase in the volume and hostility of the hecklers. They were passing a bottle of spirits around and taking large gulps. At last things calmed down enough for Philip to continue. He explained how the trade unions had begun have an effect, as in the London Docks a few years ago when their solidarity forced the employers to make improvements in their working conditions. Next, he explained how political parties had grown out of the unions until in last year's elections several members of the Labour Party had been elected to Parliament.

Now the hecklers changed their tactics. They began to hum the national anthem, softly at first, then louder. Philip tried to ignore the singing.

'A few years ago I began to work among the quarry men of North Wales.'

I noticed that his voice had filled with emotion.

'The work was incredibly difficult and dangerous. I was the medical officer and saw the most terrible injuries. And their reward for this was a pittance, which they received in the form of tokens which must be spent in their employer's shops. But that fine man Lloyd George...'

The singing of the national anthem increased in volume at the mention of this name. I had never heard of the man but the name sounded Welsh.

'forced the employers to improve the conditions and the pay.'

That drunken rabble was now singing at the tops of their voices, so that Philip had to complete his speech in almost a shout.

'Now I do not agree with everything the Liberals or the Labour Party stand for, that is why I stand as an Independent, but I can assure you that if I am elected I shall do my very best for the poorer members of our society and I shall work hard to secure votes for women.'

I was quite shocked by his last words. I knew nothing of the movement for women's suffrage, but as he gave these last words particular emphasis the singing of the national anthem ceased abruptly and angry booing began. Then the men from that part of the crowd began to surge towards the stage, forcing the audience to move, or be shoved aside, the men crying shame and the women screaming.

For a while Philip stood his ground, then a bottle was thrown at him and the portly man pulled him reluctantly off the stage. I ran forward and stood against the stage, shouting, 'How dare you! That man is my friend. He is a good, kind man.'

The men ignored me and made for the door which led backstage. I hoped that there was another way out of the building and that Philip had already escaped, but just in case I made for the door as well and stood in front of it. My anger made me foolhardy. I raised my fists ready for my second fight of the day, but now there were more than a dozen intoxicated men in front of me, some carrying bottles and baying for blood.

'OK, I'll take you one at a time.' I said, still holding my fists at the ready.

The largest of them stepped forward and swung an immense fist at me. I sidestepped in the best Southside Gymnasium manner and slammed my own fist into his chin. He looked surprised, swayed but did not fall. Instead, he took me in his huge arms, lifted me up and flung me to the floor, whereupon the others joined in by placing well aimed kicks at various parts of my anatomy. I had covered my face, but at last one of their boots got through my guard and thudded into my jaw. The pain was excruciating and I began to wonder how much longer I could go on without passing out, when I heard a shrill whistle blow somewhere nearby and my attackers scattered. I managed to turn on my side and saw a group of men in dark blue uniforms chasing them, but most of them evaded capture. Meanwhile two of the uniformed men came towards me, jerked me onto my feet, and slapped a pair of handcuffs round my wrists

It was like a nightmare. I was back on that little bridge between the straining tower and the side of the lake. Amy had fainted and was being carried away by her father and mother. I was on my way to Liverpool where I would remain in prison for almost four years.

My voice had an edge of panic in it as I began to explain.

'You don't understand...'

'Enjoying a bit of a barney were you. Well a night or two in the cells 'll cool your ardour.'

The men began to drag me away, when a voice called from the door to backstage.

'Wait!'

I knew the voice and sighed with relief.

'That man was trying to protect me against those hooligans. We heard everything. They set on him like the bunch of cowards they are. It's a group of troublemakers who follow me whenever I speak, because they know I support votes for women.'

The man who spoke next held some kind of higher rank and spoke with authority.

'Well, I don't hold with all that suffragette nonsense myself, but I believe in free speech, and if you say this man did not cause the trouble...'

'Definitely not!'

'Well then, I'll leave him to you. Remove those handcuffs constable. Goodnight gentlemen.'

As he strode away with his men behind him, I heard him mutter, 'Votes for women, indeed!'

I was feeling groggy and very sore so I lowered myself to the floor and put my head between my legs. In a daze I heard voices above me.

'Quick, Jasper. We must get this man to a seat.'

'Yes Mr Lever'

The two men lifted and half carried me through to a little room behind the stage, where they sat me down in a large chair, my face still down on my chest.

'Water, Jasper. There's a tap in that little kitchen. And cups in the cupboard. We use them for our committee meetings.'

I heard the man walk away and return quite swiftly. Then Philip knelt down and lifted my head so that I could drink. When he saw my face, he gasped and almost dropped the cup he was holding.

'My God! It's Huw! It is isn't it? What on earth...!'

Chapter Two

September 1907

When he first opened his eyes that morning John Noble did not know where he was. Light filled the room: not the soft morning glow of his South Shropshire home, but a harsh white glare, streaming in through an un-curtained window. He closed his eyes again and tried to return to sleep but the ugly clamour of strange birds in the near distance would not let him rest. The brilliant light and unusual bird cries made him wonder for a moment if he was back in Africa, where he and his first wife had spent those exciting but dangerous years as missionaries on that dark continent, before she died and he lost his faith. But they had never had a room as large as this in Africa.

He half opened his eyes again and studied the room. It was much larger than his bedroom at the school house with a high ceiling and a large window. Suddenly one of those birds he had heard in the distance came swooping towards him and landed on the window sill uttering a long plaintive call of descending, diminishing notes. It strutted along the sill on its pink legs looking in at him: a large white bird with touches of grey in its plumage and a red dot on its long white beak. He recognised the bird at once and remembered where he was. Llandudno.

The journey had been long and difficult. The train made an unscheduled stop somewhere between Wrexham and Chester- he learned later that there had been a signalling problem- so that he missed his connection and had to wait for the last Holyhead train of the day. Then there was a long wait at Llandudno junction, where he was one of only three passengers for the last connecting train. When he finally arrived at Llandudno station it was so late that there were only two cabs available; one was a motor vehicle, the other horse drawn. John did not altogether trust automobiles- he had once been left stranded half way to Shrewsbury when a friend's motor car overheated and the engine seized up - so he went to the other one and woke the driver, who had been dozing in his cab. At last they set off down Mostyn Street, clattering hooves echoing in the silence, but when they reached the small hotel in Church Walks, where he was booked in for the weekend, the place seemed to be locked up for the night. After several pulls on the bell a light came on at last in the hallway. Bolts slid back and he was admitted by a young girl, who explained to him that the proprietor had already gone to bed but they were expecting him and she would show John to his room which was on the second floor.

Too tired even to close the curtains, John took off his coat and boots, lay back on the wide bed and was soon asleep. At some time in the night he must have woken, undressed properly and slipped under the sheets. The bed was large because the room had been booked for Ella, his second wife, and himself, but at the last minute she had refused to accompany him. She hated to travel or leave the village, where her husband was the schoolmaster, but she had persuaded him to have a weekend away before the new school year began. His guilt at leaving her behind was short lived and now he was looking forward to exploring the famous North Welsh resort without having to please his wife and for a couple days free from their constant bickering.

He checked his pocket watch and discovered that it was almost time for breakfast and realised he was quite hungry. No refreshments had been available on the Holyhead train and the restaurant at Chester had closed for the night. He took another look at the room and decided it was quite unlike his expectations. The hotel had been recommended to him by a fellow sidesman at the village church; old Ebeneezer Toombs was a gloomy fellow who explained that the place was very quiet and modest, almost an annexe of the church which gave the street its name – so that John had expected a gloomy ill lit interior but the decoration, in this room at least, was bright and new. The furniture however was from an earlier era; a large oak wardrobe, a mahogany chest of drawers and a pine washstand with a marble top.

There was timid knock on the door and when he said, 'Come in' the young girl who had opened the door for him last night entered shyly, placed a jug a jug of hot water on the washstand, and hurried out again. When she had gone John got out of bed feeling that usual stiffness in his limbs which had begun to afflict him during the last few years. He remembered to close the curtains before stripping to the waist and crossing to the washstand, where he lifted the cover from the water jug, filled the basin and splashed the water onto his face. He immediately felt refreshed as he washed away the smuts from his railway journey, but when he looked in the mirror above the washstand a certain gloom descended. What an old man he had become! His still plentiful hair was quite grey, the beard below retained some colour, a brownish ginger, but the face where it showed was a gaunt mask. Oh well, he thought as he towelled himself vigorously, we cannot avoid the aging process however hard we might try.

When he had finished dressing John glanced again in the mirror, at more of a distance this time, and thought himself a little better looking, rather distinguished at least. As he walked down to the dining room he wondered what the proprietor would look like. 'Quite elderly now,' Ebeneezer had told him, 'Bit of a tartar, but very efficient. She was the widow of a vicar in the Church of Wales. A modest soul. Naturally she attracts good, churchgoing people like ourselves.'

He entered the dining room and found that it was as bright and cheerful as his bedroom and that the people filling it were mostly bright and cheerful too; several family parties with children reluctantly behaving themselves in the close company of their parents, a pair of middle-aged-women, with books beside them on the tablecloth, obviously on holiday together, possibly schoolteachers like himself. A large, florid man, in a check suit, who was ogling a young waitress and laughing loudly, as he told her some, perhaps slightly risqué, story. John wondered if the man might be a travelling salesman.

At last the proprietor appeared and came straight to John's table.

'Ah,' she said, 'You must be Mr Noble. I am sorry I wasn't able to greet you last night...' She paused, looking closely at her guest and her face began to colour up.

'Oh no, it is I who should apologise,' John said. 'My train was delayed.'

He wondered how long ago Ebeneezer had last stayed here. This was certainly not his modest, elderly vicar's widow. Here was a handsome woman in her mid-thirties he guessed, who took great care over her appearance. And there was something vaguely familiar about her.

She beckoned over one of the waitresses to take his order, then smiled and said, 'Well, Mr Noble, I hope you will have an enjoyable stay. If you are not satisfied with anything please let me know'. When she walked away between the other tables he could not help but notice what a fine figure she had. And yes, there was definitely something familiar about her

After breakfast John set off down Church Walks towards the sea. It was a splendid September morning, with tiny clouds scudding across the blue sky where gulls wheeled about on the breeze. The grey rock of the Great Orme rose sharply behind the houses on his left and the roads leading off on that side were steeply inclined. On his right the land sloped more gently down towards the town centre. He and Ella had come to Llandudno for their honeymoon about twenty-five years ago so he had some sense of the geography of the town, and remembered most of its main features, therefore he was very surprised when at the next turning on his left he discovered something that had certainly not been here when they had last visited. Here was a building of a quite unusual kind set slightly back from Church Walks. Several iron pillars held up a large roof and beneath that roof was a space where two iron rails came down to some buffers, like those at a railway station. His eyes followed the rails as they went up the steep road leading towards the summit of the Orme. When he looked up at the roof again he saw a sign announcing 'The Great Orme Tramway' and underneath the roof a line of people queued outside a ticket office. John was fascinated, even more so when a tram appeared round a corner and began to brake sharply as it came down towards the buffers. As soon as the little wooden carriage halted the driver opened a gate and stepped down from his platform at the front to allow the passengers to disembark. Most of the passengers were smiling and chattering and had obviously enjoyed the ride. When they had all left the driver closed the gate and moved along the aisle to the other end of the carriage where he opened another gate to allow his next passengers to come on board.

John hurriedly joined the queue outside the ticket office, hoping that there would be enough room left for him. Luckily there was just one seat left at the front of the carriage, when he climbed aboard, ducking his head because he was a tall man and the carriage roof was quite low.

The wooden seat was comfortable enough and the two children next to him did not take up much space, although they could not stop fidgeting, in spite of their mother's glares from her seat opposite. She relaxed a little when John smiled and said, 'It's all right, Madam. The children are naturally excited.' Then he turned away to look through the front window as the carriage began to move upwards. Now he observed that there was a third strip of iron running down the centre between the rails, in fact it was a narrow gully which guided the steel cable that was drawing them upwards. John was almost as excited as the children, but naturally at his age he had learned not to let it show.

The first part of the journey was up a very steep hill following a narrow cleft in the Orme but soon the track levelled out offering a wider view of a grass and heather covered plateau, empty except for sheep and the occasional walker who had spurned the aid of the tram. John remembered that when he had last come here this was the path he and Ella had taken to the summit. Oh, how young and healthy he had been then and how loving and lovely the new wife beside him. They had made love several times in the night and it had been a pleasant ache he had felt in his limbs next day.

Now the ache was more permanent and never caused by physical intimacy.

Often these days John felt quite breathless even when he took his daily walk up the Long Hill at the end of the school day. Once or twice, he had been forced to stop by a sharp pain in his chest. Oh well, he thought, at least I will have no problem walking back down.

Suddenly the tram slowed and a building came into view. It was like a barn with an open end. Surely, he thought, we have not reached the summit already. The woman opposite must have seen the puzzled look on his face.

'This is the half-way point. We have to change carriages here.'

'Oh, I see. Thank you.'

Already the children were clambering over him to get off. The women spoke sharply to them. She seemed to be having trouble controlling her offspring. He glanced again at the woman and realised that she was quite young, in her mid-twenties at most and very pretty. He wondered where her husband was. There was no indication that she was a widow. She was well-dressed, well-spoken and, he guessed, quite well-off. Perhaps her husband was abroad in a part of the ever-expanding Empire, but if he was a diplomat of some kind surely the woman would have a companion with her, or at least a Nanny to keep an eye on the children, who were both under five years old. He was curious but he would never have the courage to ask. He decided however that he must change seats for the next part of the journey.

At last the tram reached the summit and he stood for a while, simply admiring the view. To the east, across the Conway estuary, the mountains of Snowdonia were half hidden in customary clouds. Southwards he saw Anglesey. Out to the west the sun sparkled on the sea in the clear air and that distant smudge on the horizon might even be the Isle of Man. Northwards as he looked across the town towards the Little Orme at the other end of the bay he became aware of how much the town had developed since his last visit. Now houses stretched almost from the North Shore to the West Shore. And there was change much nearer at hand. During that last visit with Ella the only building up here at the summit had been a signalling station helping the vessels down there on the sea to make a safe journey. Now this was being demolished and he discovered that a large hotel was to be built on the site. He rather disapproved. Surely it would mean that this would become just another place for the better off to have a good time rather than a windswept wilderness to be explored by anyone who made the effort.

He walked down the western slope towards St Tudno's church and sat on the springy turf above the graveyard. There was a time he knew when this was the main church for the people of Llandudno who had to climb all the way up here to worship. He thought about his own church back in the village of Hope Underhill and how his own attitude to religion had changed in recent years. In his youth he had become an atheist: partly because he had read The Origin of Species and saw how it made nonsense of the Old Testament story; partly because of his disillusion with missionary work in Africa; but his views were confirmed when he discovered that the incumbent of the parish of Hope Underhill had murdered his predecessor at the local school, a young woman called Harriet Owen. John had been one of the first to discover her corpse in a barley field and had continued to investigate her murder long after the police had given up. Eventually he unmasked the rector who was later hanged at Shrewsbury Gaol.

The problem he faced was that he was Headmaster of a Church School and if he was to keep his post he had to continue to pretend that he was a committed Christian and attend the parish church regularly. He had explained his view of religion to Amy, his stepdaughter, of whom he was very fond. When she grew into a young woman she accused him of hypocrisy, but he explained his predicament and she had understood.

It was when Amy ran off with a young Welsh quarryman and bore his child that John's view of religion began to change. He had cast out Amy from his home and a few years later she had died of poverty and disease. He began to wonder whether his stepdaughter would have been so rebellious if he had not poisoned her mind against religion.

Now after all these years the regularity and familiarity of worship at the parish church had become a comfort. He had not really become a believer but got tremendous relief from the coming together with his fellow worshippers to partake in the services each Sunday. He would look around at the ancient stones of the church, the coloured windows glowing in the morning light, the flickering candles at evensong and the contented faces of his fellow parishioners. He enjoyed singing the well-known hymns and repeating the prayers he knew off by heart. He liked the present Rector who had been here for many years and enjoyed his very practical homilies. Recently John had been made a sidesman, a great honour, and he had been appointed to the Parish Council. Perhaps it was all nonsense, but it certainly gave shape and purpose to his life.

He sat in the sunshine looking down at the neat little church and its well-kept graveyard, hearing the shush of the sea on the cliffs below and the gulls wailing above him and wondered if perhaps there was a God after all.

The death of her beloved daughter had had the opposite effect upon Ella. She had not dared to stop her husband when he turned away her pregnant daughter away from their door, thinking that there would soon be reconciliation, but Amy had disappeared and when, five years later Ella herself had discovered her daughter dead on the shores of Lake Vyrnwy she had turned against her husband and her religion. No God could allow that to happen and no father, or stepfather, should have caused it to happen. She had taken Amy's child into her own home and had never entered the church again.

John was so deep in thought that he did not at first notice that he had company and it was obvious that the company had not noticed him. He kept very still and watched as a young couple walked through the churchyard with arms entwined, while two young children gambolled about among the gravestones, their disrespect ignored by the grownups who were totally immersed in themselves. He recognised the woman immediately, but he did not think that the man, who now embraced her passionately, was her husband. Well, well, well. He was glad when they had gone, still not noticing him, and he decided that it was time for him to move on.

When he returned to the boarding house for lunch the landlady did not appear. His walk had given him a good appetite but afterwards he began to feel quite tired. This was something else he had noticed recently, this desire to have a snooze after lunch. It was a terrible admission to make but occasionally he had drifted off in the classroom in the afternoon, when the children were busy with their arithmetic or compositions. So far none of his pupils seemed to have noticed and when the shuffle of a chair or a cough woke him again they were all still hard at work. Over the years he had gained respect and discipline was easy, after all some of the children in the Infants room next door were the grandchildren of those he had taught so many years ago. Now he made his way to the sitting room, was glad to find it empty, slumped into one of the easy chairs, covered his face with a newspaper and soon fell asleep.

'Mr Noble...Mr Noble!' He woke abruptly to find the landlady smiling down at him. The newspaper had slipped from his face.

'Oh, I'm so sorry to have woken you, but I had to speak to you while you were on your own.'

John sat up, still rather dazed. The woman pulled up another chair in front of him, saying, 'You don't recognise me, do you?'

'Well I...'

'Beatrice...Beatrice Hardy. Well that was my name then. I was one of your pupils, and a great friend of Amy's.'

'Beatrice, of course...' John remembered her now. A small slim shy girl with long dark hair who followed Amy everywhere. He found it hard to reconcile that memory with the handsome, confident woman in front of him now.

'I married a farmer from near Bishopton. Ted Lewis. He was a good deal older than me. He died three year ago. Left me the farm, but I couldn't manage it by myself, so I sold up and bought this hotel.'

'You seem to be doing well.'

'Oh yes. Of course, I had to make changes. Very run down it was, quite gloomy and, frankly, rather filthy. I don't think the old woman could see very well. Now we're full most of the time.' Then she added in a different tone, 'I was dreadfully upset when I heard about Amy'

'Yes. It was a difficult time.'

'You have taken on her little daughter, I believe.'

'Yes...Nan, but she is no longer little. She is seventeen.'

'Well, that must be some comfort, I mean, after losing Amy.

John felt so many feelings whirling around, but certainly no comforting ones. He answered in a dead tone, 'Yes' but the woman, Beatrice, did not seem to notice. Instead she smiled brightly, blushing slightly.

'Shall I tell you a secret?'

John frowned, wondering what was coming

'When I was at school, in the last couple of years, I had a... crush...I think they call it, on you. I thought you were wonderful'

Now it was John's turn to blush.

'I was so jealous of Amy, having you as a stepfather. I liked Amy, but I hung around with her mainly because I thought I would see more of you. Of course, you hardly noticed me. And Amy was so beautiful...and clever. I was nothing next to her.'

'Well, you have done very well for yourself, haven't you? And you have kept your looks. Amy may have been beautiful and clever as you say. But it all came to nothing because she wouldn't listen to me.'

'I never really knew what had happened. Only that she had died.'

'I'm sorry. I'd rather not go into it. It was a long time ago. Let me just enjoy my little holiday at your excellent hotel.'

The woman stared at him in silence for a while, then spoke softly, 'Yes, you're right. It wasn't fair of me to ask. But it is wonderful to see you again. Perhaps we can talk again for a while before you leave? You can tell me all about life in Hope Underhill. D'you know, I haven't been back there in more than ten years.'

'Of course.' John pulled himself up out of his chair. 'But I'm not going to enjoy my holiday, if I spend it asleep. I really must walk down to the sea front and get some fresh air.'

'Well, I'll see you this evening, John. May I call you that?' she said and moved away with the grace and posture of a still quite young woman, giving him a little wave.

Yes, he thought, I'd like that. Then he set off for the seafront.

As he walked down Church Walks towards the Parade he thought briefly about Ella and wondered if he should send her a postcard, but as he was going back home on Monday he would probably be there before it arrived. And perhaps it would only remind her of their happier days. Since Amy's death she had aged rapidly, her figure sagging, her face quite lined and her once golden hair thinner now and threaded with silver. He could not help but compare her with Beatrice; her splendid figure, her smooth round face and glossy brown hair. He still could not believe that this woman was that mousy little girl who followed Amy everywhere. He blushed again at her admission of a 'crush' on him.

Even late in the season the parade was crowded. Children were gathered round the little booth watching Punch knocking Judy about. There was more laughter from the adults than the children who seemed rather worried about what was happening and kept glancing at their parents for reassurance before smiling slightly. During recent years John had sometimes felt like giving Ella a slap for her moroseness and cold manner towards him, but he had never actually raised his hand.

Ever since Amy's daughter Nan had come into their lives she had become the centre of Ella's world. John found her less easy to like, with her dark looks, her secretive nature and her eyes that glittered with intelligence and sometimes seemed to look right through him. But the main problem for John was that the girl was a constant reminder of her father, that young Welshman who had charmed them all, even taken them to stay briefly at his home in the mountains, then abducted and raped his stepdaughter with all the tragic consequences which had followed.

Now the centre of John's world was his son, a fine looking young man, also called John, sometimes still called 'little' John, though now he was taller than his father, and who would soon be going back to Cambridge for his final year. He had been away for a few weeks staying with a friend from his college who lived near Salisbury, but he would be home again when John returned tomorrow. The boy had been a late developer and there had been times when he was a small boy that his father worried about his academic progress, but suddenly, rather strangely, from the moment his sister disappeared he had changed his temperament and become a good scholar, soon outstripping his father, so that he was able to obtain a scholarship to a local public school. Since those early days father and son had got on swimmingly and John was sure that his son would become a man of real note in the world.

His thoughts were disturbed, and his heart jumped, when a loud 'parp...parp!' sounded behind him and he turned to see one of those damned automobiles forcing its way through the crowd. Once he had been all for progress, but these noisy, smelly vehicles with their arrogant drivers just annoyed him. They represented unacceptable change. Suddenly he felt oppressed by the crowd and pushed his way down the steps to the beach. The tide was out and there was much activity on the trampled sand. Donkeys ambled back and forth, led by the donkey lady or one of her youthful assistants, while the children sitting astride those placid beasts smiled smugly at their waiting parents. Other children were building sandcastles or burying their fathers who were sleeping off their lunchtime ale. At the edge of the sea barefooted little girls lifted their dresses, stepped into the tiny waves, screamed and stepped back again.

John moved away from the crowded end of the beach and followed the lacy fringe of the waves towards the Little Orme. After a while the sand gave way to pebbles and walking became more laborious, but soon he reached another stretch of sand, which he had almost to himself. He stopped to examine a jelly fish, turning it over with his stick and examining its slimy tentacles. Then he saw an interesting shell and turned to show it to Amy, as he had so often pointed out things of interest to her on their walks together long ago. He felt his eyes smart and told himself it was the salty air.

Looking seawards he saw a steamboat making its way towards the end of the pier. Twice a day such boats brought hundreds of visitors from Liverpool, a place he had never visited, but had often thought about. He remembered the doctor he had met at Vyrnwy, during that fateful visit. Dr Lever had come from Liverpool to see the completion of the dam he had worked so hard to have built, which would hold back the water until it formed a lake to provide good drinking water for his home city. He had brought his son with him and they had stayed with friends at their home overlooking the valley, which the lake was soon to fill. The son, Phillip, was a tall, handsome, educated young man, destined to follow his father into the medical profession.

He had instantly fallen for Amy and John thought him a very suitable suitor for her in a year or two. But she was not interested in him, preferring that Welshman, with his labourer's body and rough hands; Huw Morris, who was dark and squat, who lived in the back of beyond and had no prospects at all.

When the police had rescued Amy from the Straining Tower at the edge of the filling lake, they had taken Huw to a prison in Liverpool. The main charge he faced was being part of a group of

Welsh activists who had attempted to blow up the tunnel which would take the water under the Berwyn Mountains to Liverpool via Oswestry. John had not pressed any charges against Huw, partly because Amy had gone with him willingly but mainly because she was quite unwell for a while and there was no way her parents wanted her travelling to Liverpool and appearing in court. It was only when Amy told them that she was pregnant and John threw her out of their home that he thought of making further accusations against Huw, but by that time Amy had disappeared.

John had not kept in touch with the Levers' or followed up the case against Huw, except when the court proceedings against him were recorded in the newspaper and he learned that Huw had received a custodial sentence. There had been no news about him ever since.

John had been so occupied with these thoughts that he did not realise how far he had walked, stumbling along through alternating patches of pebbles and soft sand. Then he felt that slight ache again in his chest. He looked inland and discovered that he had walked beyond the last of the hotels. He climbed back onto the promenade and rested while the sun sank towards the sea. Then he consulted his pocket watch and decided that if he walked back slowly, he would be in time for the evening meal. The sea air had certainly given him an appetite and he would be pleased to see Beatrice again.

Chapter Three

The evening meal was excellent; Windsor soup, roast lamb and a sticky chocolate pudding. John had not had such an appetite for years. The sea air was doing him good. The only disappointment was that Beatrice did not appear. As the waitress cleared his table John asked, 'Is Mrs Lewis not with us this evening?'

'No, Sir. She's gone to a concert at the Pavilion. With that Mr Baines. You know, the man who sits at that table in the corner. Always laughing and joking he is.'

The look on the waitresses face showed that she did not approve of Mr Baines.

'I see...'

Apparently he's got connections with the management. They give him...what d'you call them?'

'Complimentary tickets?'

'That's right. He asked me to go last week. But I wouldn't. Even though it was my night off.'

'You don't like Mr Baines?

'Well, I don't have the right to like or not like him. He's a guest. So that's that. Mind you I don't blame Mrs Lewis for going. She deserves a treat. She works so hard. And she knows how to look after herself.'

The waitress smiled conspiratorially, then walked quickly away with the pile of dishes.

So, no tete-a-tete with Beatrice this evening. Perhaps tomorrow? John took his coffee into the sitting room. Most of the guests had gone out again. It was still a lovely evening. The band would be playing on the promenade. And there would be a concert party in the Happy Valley. The only other people in the room were the two single ladies, sitting side by side on a small settee. They looked up briefly when he said good evening, gave him a look of contempt and returned to their animated conversation. John picked a book off the shelves and sat as far away as he could from these ladies, but continued to observe them over his volume and to listen in to their conversation.

The older of the two women, in her thirties perhaps, was quite masculine in her features and very plainly dressed, in sombre tones with no hint of frills or flounces. Her companion was few years younger and rather more feminine in looks and dress, even quite pretty, but without the obvious sexual charm of someone like Beatrice. The older woman was speaking in a low gruff voice.

'Such a delightful journey. Especially from Llangollen. I'm so glad we decided to take that route.'

'Oh yes, Llangollen was delightful. With that ruined abbey in the valley and the castle on the hill, but especially Plas Newydd. I really loved it there. I could quite imagine those ladies sitting in their garden.'

'Mmm, Lady Eleanor and her beloved Sarah. What courage they must have had to defy everyone and set up home together.

'If only...'

'But of course they had the means...'

'Oh Marion, do you think we could ever...'

The younger woman began to sob. Her companion leant over and whispered softly, 'Kitty, my dear, you are such a soft sweet girl. But it's what I love about you.'

John watched the older woman's hand cover the small pale fingers of her companion as she looked into her eyes.

He snapped his book shut, stood up and left the room. He heard them laughing together as he walked up the stairs.

He checked his watch. It was only nine o'clock, but the previous late night and the long active day which followed had exhausted him, so he drew the curtains, undressed and lay back on the bed. He thought about the women in the sitting room. He knew that there were women who preferred their own sex. Just as there were men similarly inclined. There had been the notorious trial of

Oscar Wilde just a few years ago. He had known men like that too. In fact he had experienced that feeling very briefly when he had been at boarding school, with a boy called Charles Ingram, a pretty blonde boy at that time, who went on to be a respected Member of Parliament, but John had soon known that he preferred women. He began to think back to the women he had known in that way.

The first had been an itinerant labourer on his father's farm. She had come from over the Welsh border to help with the harvest. He had just come down from university and had got engaged to his first wife, but Elizabeth, his fiancé, who came from a strict non-conformist background was rather straight laced and would not allow any physical intimacy until they were married. She had spent some of the vacation with him on the farm and when she had gone home again he felt very frustrated.

To deal with his frustration John decided to help with harvest. His eyes soon strayed to the women working alongside him and especially to this brown skinned, black eyed Welshwoman, who soon made it obvious that she had noticed him. The woman was several years his senior, not particularly beautiful, perhaps not even very clean, but she exuded sexuality in a way he had never experienced before. At the end of one long hot day, when the others harvesters had all gone home, she had followed him into the wood beside the field where he had gone to relieve himself. Soon they were lying together among the wheat straw, where she had lifted her skirts, opened her bare legs and let him enter her.

Filled with guilt he had left the farm next day and gone on a walking tour of Snowdonia.

When his training as a missionary was completed he married Elizabeth and as they travelled south along the African coast she gradually accepted his advances with slightly more enthusiasm but, John suspected, more for the hope that it would lead to conception rather than any inherent pleasure. When the conceptions led only to a series of miscarriages and his wife's health declined their intimacy ceased. John began to seek satisfaction among the uninhibited African women instead.

With Ella his second wife it had been quite different. She was a lovely healthy young woman who not only allowed frequent intercourse but often instigated it. After all she had been widowed at a very early age and had missed out on sexual fulfilment for a number of years. For a while they had a very good physical relationship and eventually this resulted in the birth of their son. Here the troubles began. The baby had been sickly and required Ella's full attention. Then she had suffered an early menopause which left her ill-tempered and frigid. There were still rare times after this when they came together but these became less frequent and after the death of Amy they ceased all together.

With all these thoughts of sex John became slightly aroused, but soon his weariness took over and he fell into a light sleep. In his dreams he entered a bedroom where a woman lay in a large bed facing away from him. He lifted the counterpane and slipped in beside her. He moved slowly closer and put his arm around her warm body. Her nightdress had ridden up and he put a hand on her thigh. She moaned and turned to face him. He was shocked to discover that it was Amy, his stepdaughter, smiling at him. He jerked awake and heard someone tapping on the bedroom door. He had not locked the door so he called softly, 'Come in.'

The door opened and Beatrice entered carrying a candle. She was wearing a pale blue nightdress of some flimsy material which revealed her figure. Her hair hung loosely over her shoulders. She set the candle down on the chest of drawers and came towards the bed, where she sat looking down at him. John was shocked and delighted at the same time. He sat up and faced this handsome woman and made the silly gesture of pulling the bedclothes higher. The woman smiled and spoke softly, 'John, my dear, I so much wanted to continue our conversation, but that buffoon Baines, invited me to the concert. He's a very generous customer so I could not really refuse, and the pavilion orchestra is really top notch these days. But here I am jabbering on about myself when I really wanted to find out about you. So how are things between you and your wife?'

Still being half asleep John found himself being more honest than he intended. 'We...We do not get on that well, I suppose.'

'Ah,' said Beatrice, 'I did wonder when she did not accompany you. Of course at first you were just Mr and Mrs Noble, but when I realised who you were, I was pleased she had not come.'

'Ella does not like travelling. She won't even go to Shrewsbury unless it is absolutely necessary.'

'You don't have much in common any more'

This was a statement rather than a question.

'I suppose not. How did you know?'

'Because I recognise loneliness when I see it. I have been lonely myself"

'You mean after Ted died?'

'Oh, no, long before that.'

She shifted closer to him on the bed and took one of his hands in hers.

'You see, Ted was much older than me. I was just nineteen when he asked me to marry him. He was a good, kind man, but already in his fifties. He had made a success of the farm and was quite well off, but the effort had made him old before his time.

'So why did you accept him.'

'Well, I was no beauty then, certainly not like your Amy. I seem to have grown into my looks as the years have passed.'

John studied the woman in front of him. In the candle light her skin seemed young and healthy and as she leant forward her ample bosom showed itself through the thin fabric of her nightdress. Yes, she had certainly improved with age from that pale, skinny little schoolgirl he could just remember. He also remembered that she had not been particularly bright. She went on.

'I was just an ordinary village girl. Not clever enough to go on studying. When I first left school my mother was glad of my help with the younger children but then they grew up and she didn't need me anymore. But money was scarce. If I didn't marry somebody then I would have had to go into service. I did have a couple of proposals but they were just the usual village lads with nothing to recommend them. So when I met Ted, at one of those harvest does in the village and he seemed to like me I just went along with it. After all to be mistress of a large house and married to a man of substance...Well I thought that might make up for...other things.

'Hmm...'

And Ted was good to me. He taught me so much. How to run the household. How to treat your employees. How the world of business worked. All the things that have helped me here. And I suppose...'

'What?'

'Well, if we'd had children it might have worked better. But Ted was not often up to it...If you know what I mean. And on the rare occasions that he was, well, nothing came of it.'

By now John had an erection, not as strong as in his younger days, but it made him want to undo those ribbons on her nightdress.

'So there I was, still a young woman, up in that big house among the hills, feeling hot and bothered whenever one of the strong, healthy workers came near me. Then Ted became ill and we couldn't even share the social events and the Sunday jaunts any more. I certainly knew loneliness then.'

John smiled to imagine what Ebeneezer would think of this scene. Instead of a skinny old martinet of a proprietor, probably peering at him through a lorgnette as he struggled through a tough steak here was this handsome, warm blooded woman sitting close to him on his bed holding his hand. Beatrice noticed the smile and asked, 'What is it, John?'

'Nothing, my dear' He leant forward and kissed her on the cheek. She returned the kiss on his lips and pulled at the ribbon at her throat so that the nightdress became loose and slipped off her shoulders. The figure that was revealed was magnificent, shapely breasts still firm because they had never nursed children and with large dark nipples. He reached out and touched one with the back of his hand. Beatrice gasped and stood up so that the nightdress fell off her completely. His erection was now quite firm. He lifted the bedclothes to let the naked woman join him. She pulled his nightshirt over his head and studied his thin chest where the ribs showed clearly and the hairs were greying. He knew that she was seeing an old man and knew that he had to prove that he was still young at heart. He raised himself so that she was underneath him, her legs spread, and pushed his member towards her, but already the erection was going, the member wilting. He collapsed onto her and began to sob.

She took his head in her hands and held him.

'John, dear. It's not your fault. This was wrong of me. I was full of my memories of you as my beloved teacher: when you were tall and strong, with your thick dark hair and your curly beard. I still had my schoolgirl admiration and silly schoolgirl dreams. But I see now that you too are getting old. It wasn't fair of me to expect...I'll leave you now.'

She quickly rose from his bed, put on her nightdress and left the room. The forgotten candle sputtered in the draught her exit caused.

John immediately regretted that he had allowed her into his room and what had so nearly taken place. Oh, my God, what would happen if Beatrice, in her disappointment, decided to be malicious and tell Ella or make it known among the people of Hope Underhill. Everything he had strived for would crumble away; his reputation, his career, his status in the church. And his fall would inevitably taint his son.

Very early next morning John dressed, went quietly downstairs, slowly eased back the bolts, and left the hotel. He would walk to the station and catch the earliest train. The weather had changed, with grey clouds looming and a chill breeze coming off the sea. The streets were empty on this early Sunday morning.

When he reached the station he discovered that the first train would not be leaving for another hour, so he made his way back to the sea front and sat on one of the new benches that lined the promenade. The tide was nearly full and waves were rolling in, dumping themselves on the beach and dragging the pebbles down the slope. Several small boats were already bobbing about on the swell while others lined up near a jetty to wait for those brave enough to take a trip round the bay.

Soon it was time to make his way back to the station. John took one last look out to sea and there on the distant horizon he saw a ship passing. Even from this distance he could tell that it was a very large ship and its four tall funnels told him that must be one of those amazing ocean liners that were just going into service for the Cunard Line. He had read about them in his newspaper and there had been photographs too. The ships had strange names...Lusitania was it...and Mauretania...sounding like exotic countries in one of those musical comedies that were so popular nowadays. He had been fascinated to read that these ships were nearly 800 feet long and ten storeys high, so that there were electric lifts to transport the passengers up and down. The ships were powered by steam turbines and the hulls were divided into watertight compartments so that even if one section was damaged the rest would remain afloat, thus making them unsinkable. The ships were so luxurious that it was like being in the grandest hotel. The ship he saw now must have just left Liverpool and was travelling very quickly southwards, smoke and steam pouring out of its four funnels and streaming behind. Perhaps it was undergoing sea- trials or even perhaps making its maiden voyage to the United States of America.

Chapter Four

When we reached the Adelphi I asked Philip to wait in the lounge, while I went up to my room to make repairs to my face and change into my evening wear. When I returned Philip just gaped at my expensive clothes. I led him to the dining room and took the table reserved for me. Immediately a waiter hurried over, bowed slightly, and looked rather askance at my companion who in his opinion was not suitably attired. I laughed to myself and, when the waiter had left us, chuckled out loud.

'He is inclined to think that you are not suitably dressed for the Adelphi'

Philip continued to stare open mouthed at my transformation, so I tried to put him at his ease.

'So you wish to become a Member of Parliament?'

'Yes, but there's little hope of my being elected. I am considered too radical. Especially with my views on women's suffrage'

'How did that happen?'

'Well I suppose, in a way, you are to blame.'

'Me?'

'Yes. It began when I went to see how your family were getting on without you at Ty Craig. Of course the place was deserted, so I went on to the slate quarry to find out where they had gone.'

'Yes, I remember. Then you became the medical officer and you saw how badly the quarrymen were treated. I knew that long ago. When you got me released from jail'

'My experience at the quarry told me that things had to change, as I said in my speech. And I had to change first. So I gave away my expensive clothes and took to wearing more workmanlike clothing, like this.'

I studied his rough tweed suit. It was a made of a tough material which would almost outlast him and in a colours that would barely show any dirt. The cut and cloth of the suit went well with his strong features and wiry frame.

'I gave up all that artistic nonsense – landscape photography and such like- though I still occasionally took photographs of the men working in the quarry, so that I could show how hard and dangerous was their task, and to show their injuries when I tried to gain some compensation from their employers. And I tried to learn the language of my patients.

'Pwy dach chi?' I asked to test him and he came back straight away with, 'Philip dew i'

His pronunciation was good, for an Englishman. I returned to English, not sure how well I could continue in Welsh after so many years. He went on to tell me how he had become estranged from his father, who did not like his new political attitude.

'Is Joseph still alive? 'I asked.

'No. He died several years ago.'

I was sorry about that. Joseph had been a good man. Even though he had helped to steal that Welsh valley by filling it with water for the use of his own English city.

'And why are you in favour of giving women the vote?'

'Because I now share the view of someone we both knew many years ago. Women must have more control of their destiny if they are ever to improve their lives.'

I was about to ask who that woman was when the waiter arrived with our meal. I told him that my companion was about to become a Member of Parliament. His attitude changed slightly, but he was still not convinced about the clothes. He asked me to test the wine. I recognised it at once as a fine claret. Julia had taught me about such things. Philip took a sip from his own glass and was obviously impressed.

As the waiter walked away Philip said, 'Look, that's quite enough about me. I long to hear your story. It must be quite extraordinary. I mean when I last saw you boarding ship on that cold, wet day you were dressed almost in rags and had only enough money to pay for your passage and perhaps to live for a few days in New York.'

'And even that was due to you, Philip. I shall never forget your kindness. First you rescued me from that awful jail, then helped me to emigrate. I can never repay you.'

'Well I won't accept your money, but you can repay me nevertheless.'

'How?'

'By telling me your story'

'Very well.'

I did not dwell on the voyage, except to mention briefly the crowded, unsanitary conditions, the obvious poverty of my fellow emigrants wherever they came from, which was mainly Russia, Poland, Czechoslovakia as well as Ireland, the terrible storms, and a near collision with another vessel in thick fog. I told him of the resentment those of us from the lower deck felt when we lined up to be immunised while the first and second class passengers looked on.

But the majority of us felt our spirits rise when at last we entered New York harbour and saw that gigantic Statue of Liberty rising from the water as a symbol of hope for us all. However our humiliations were not over. Soon we were transferred to smaller ships and taken across to Ellis Island. Actually one of our number chose to jump into the sea instead and swim for the mainland, but he didn't get very far before some men in a rowing boat picked him up. He was a strange man. I had noticed him on the voyage, very tall and thin, dressed in black clothes that were too small for him. I never saw him eat or drink, or take any exercise. Each day he sat in the same place on the deck, clutching a small black bag, the same bag he was still carrying when he jumped overboard. I never discovered what was in the bag because as those men rowed towards him he threw the bag into the water. Whatever it contained must have been heavy because the bag immediately sank beneath the waves.

I don't know what happened to the man. I never saw him or heard of him again.

When I landed on Ellis Island I was one of thousands, crammed into a huge building where we were examined medically, with about as much humanity as the beasts in Dolgellau market, and interrogated by various officials (whose questions I had to answer several times before they could understand my accent) but finally I was given permission to enter the United States of America. Of course not everyone made it. There were some who were rejected, for whatever reason, and sent back on the next boat to where they had come from. But I was allowed to continue and soon found myself walking the streets of Manhattan.

I can truly say that I had never felt so small or lost in my life. Partly it was grid system of the streets themselves. I don't know whether you know this but the streets of that city are built to a plan, each street is perfectly straight and is criss-crossed by other streets at perfect right angles, and the streets do not have names, such as Lime Street or Vauxhall Road, instead they are named abstractly, as East Forty Second Street or Fifth Avenue.

Next it was a mass of traffic and people crowding the streets. When I first arrived in New York all the traffic was still horse drawn: huge loaded wagons as well as carriages, carts and cabs. Some of the less crowded streets were lined with fine mansions where the well-off strolled along the wide sidewalks – that's what the pavements are called over there- or rode in open carriages so that they could be admired in their fine clothes. Other streets, the ones I was to live among, were narrower, meaner, filled with the greatest mix of people you ever saw. It is said that all Americans are immigrants and that is how it seemed to me during those first days. We think of Liverpool as cosmopolitan and indeed it is, but, do y'know, there were some streets over there where almost every person, man, women or child was black, or in other streets, Chinese or in another, obviously Jewish with all the men in black clothes and with long black beards. I suppose I felt most at home among the streets where the Irish brogue prevailed, so there I sought lodging, with the few dollars I had been given in exchange for what remained of the money you had loaned to me.

The O'Malley's, my landlords, were a strange couple. She was enormous, with muscular arms and hands like a bare-knuckle fighter. She wore the same dress every day and never apparently washed – there was a tap in the back yard but nowhere in the whole house where you could wash in private- so that a strong odour of un-washed woman preceded her everywhere. Her face might once have been pleasing, for she had well shaped lips, fine white teeth and eyes as blue as a spring sky, but now the folds of flesh on her neck and cheeks trembled as she moved, like pink blancmange. Her name was Maeve.

Mr O'Malley on the other hand was small and neat and his dark eyes flickered about the world like those of a cornered rat. He worked at the harbour, though his wife would have been better I'm sure at humping those huge sacks that came up from the ship's holds. Every night when he came home he drank himself insensible, but never seemed to have a problem getting up next morning.

The most astonishing thing about them both was the great love they showed for one another. He always had a soft word for his Maeve and she would hug him at times with such ferocity that I was sure might one day be fatal. And this intimacy obviously continued when they were in bed, for they had several children, running wild about the place.

I wondered how such a couple could have afforded to own such a large house, but one day Samuel, that was O'Malley's name, explained to me that his wife came from a well off family and when she eloped with him she had taken most of the family silver with her.

'I'd have murdered them all and stolen everything for my dear Samuel,' she asserted, when I questioned her.

My room had two advantages. Firstly it was right at the top of the house, which afforded me some privacy and secondly it was very cheap. But the disadvantages were considerable; the room was very small, damp, and dirty and the bed harboured an army of fleas. But I had no chance of moving on until I had found work.

This did not prove easy at all. You see, what I didn't know and nobody bothered to tell me was that the American economy had collapsed in the previous year. It started with the railroads, which had been overbuilt, and several became bankrupt. There was a panic and people took their money out of the banks, so they crashed. This was followed by a credit squeeze which caused thousands of companies to go out of business.

The problem for me was that my only real skill was fixing explosive into a mountainside, setting it off and causing a landslide of slate. Here in New York there were no mountainsides and any slate for rooftops had to be imported, usually from Wales.

I was down to my last few cents and living largely on food from charity hand-outs, and the patience of my landlords who saw me as a good tenant- that is I didn't drink too much or fight or steal - and were prepared to wait a while for my rent, when my luck suddenly changed, but at someone else's expense.

There was this street market nearby, where I often walked in the hope of finding some fruit that had fallen off a stall. My eyes were on the ground as I walked along but I suddenly heard this scream and looked up to see that a man had fallen in the road and his leg had been crushed by a passing cart. A couple of his companions tried to lift him and carry him to the nearest hospital, but they couldn't manage it on their own. I joined them and between us we managed to get him to where his injuries could be dealt with. He had passed out on the way, but the surgeon assured his friends that his leg could be mended but it would be ages before the man would be mobile again. Outside the hospital the men thanked me for my help and I began to walk away. Then one of them called me back.

'D'you need a job, lad.'

I told him that I certainly did.

'Well, we're a team, you see, and now we're a man down, so we could use a fit young guy like yourself, 'til Seamus is fit again.'

'What is it you do?' I asked.

'We collect the garbage from the market and take it to the nearest dump. We have a small cart. One of us pulls the cart while the others load the waste. Of course the stuff stinks, and you get it all over you.'

He held out an arm to me and it did indeed smell foul.

'But we can make a living. We split the cash between us at the end of the day. There won't be much because we shall want to give Seamus a small share to keep him going till he's back on his feet, but it's a job and that's better than nothing.'

So I spent a couple of months shovelling a stinking mix of food waste and horse shit into that small cart and pushing it to the tip and had enough at the end of each week to pay my rent and buy a small amount of food. And while we were making one of our journeys to the tip I had another bit of luck. We were passing a large hole in the ground where the sewers were being extended when someone like a foreman was sacking one of the workers. We stopped to watch and the foreman saw us.

'What the 'ell are you lot looking at. He's useless. Too bloody weak to lift a shovel let alone use it.'

The man had wandered away. The foreman looked at me.

'You look as if you could handle a shovel. Do you want his job?'

I had lost a lot of my strength in jail and while sailing across the ocean, but my recent work with the cart had helped me regain some of my fitness. I turned to my friends and shrugged, but one of them said, 'Take it. We didn't know how to tell you, but Seamus is coming back next week.'

So now I was shovelling dirt instead of waste, but the pay was better and the foreman seemed satisfied with my work, so for another few months I helped to improve the sewerage system of

New York. Then I spotted another opportunity on one of the innumerable building sites where the older original buildings were being replaced by larger, higher ones. They were looking for someone with explosives experience. I applied and got the job. At last I was working in the open air and doing work I could do well. Of course the work was hard and many of my fellow workers were not much better than beasts, but compared with my homeland, the wages were enough to give me a reasonable life. The first thing I did when I had saved a little from my wages was to buy a better mattress and sneak the old one down stairs, when the O'Malley's were asleep or too busy making more children, and carry it to the nearest dump. Then, after thoroughly fumigating my room, I had an itch-free night for the first time in nearly a year. After that I began to save a small amount each week for some future project that was not yet clear in my mind.

I cannot say that I liked New York. Too many people crowded into a small space. Too much brick and concrete and hardly a green space to be seen, well at least in my part of the city. In winter the city was astonishingly cold, with chilling winds that howled down the straight streets and in summer the winds would drop completely and the streets would become airless cauldrons. There was also a high level of crime and violence, partly because of the crowded nature of the city, but also because of antagonism between one nationality and another. But I got used to the work and began to know a few people and sometimes joined them in a nearby bar. I was careful not to drink too much or spend too much. But I enjoyed their talk of other parts of this vast country they had visited. Perhaps one day I would visit some of those places, but as yet I hadn't the courage. At least in New York I had a humble home and steady work, so I stuck it out for a couple of years.

But things suddenly began to change. O'Malley lost his job. Apparently he tried to lift too large a load and his back gave way. There was no sympathy from his bosses. After a few days absence he was sacked. To keep the wolf from the door Maeve decided to increase the income from lodgers. I was asked to share.

My new roommate was strange man. He was from somewhere in Poland and had a name I could barely say, let alone spell. He rarely spoke and even when he did I found it impossible to understand him. His silence in the day he made up for with the noise he made at night; his snores were so loud it seemed to me the walls shook. I was back to sleepless nights and weary days. It was time to move on.

Chapter Five

When John Noble left the train at Churchtown and began the steep climb up onto the Long Hill, which he must cross in order get home, the guilt returned. In his mind he had committed adultery and, even though his body had not performed the act, he had broken his marriage vows. Of course it was worrying that he had been unable to go through with it – what was the cause of that he wondered?- but far more to the point was this: what if Beatrice decided to be vindictive or perhaps just careless and let it be known what had nearly occurred and news got back here? How would he be able to face Ella and his fellow villagers then? He knew from his newspaper that morals had become lax in the last few years, but a village like Hope Underhill was at least fifty years behind the times.

At last he reached the top of the steep hill and stopped to gather his breath. He had decided not to hire a lift but to walk the three miles to Hope Underhill, even though he was carrying a small suitcase, so that had time to think things out. The weather had improved as he travelled back from the Welsh coast, so that now he was walking in late morning sun shine. There was rarely any traffic on this lonely road, especially on a Sunday, but if anyone rode by and offered him a lift he would say that he preferred to walk. The bracken on the hill was turning to a dull gold in contrast to the dark green pools of whinberry bushes. In the distance he could see a group of wild ponies, outlined in the sunlight, munching the turf and flicking their tails.

Of course it would be good to see his son again and discuss with

him the coming year at university and what career he thought he might follow once his studies were over. He had been studying the sciences and was hoping to go on to do research if he did well in his examinations. His father thoroughly approved of this. He had himself been interested in science as a younger man but now the rapid changes in science rather baffled and perhaps even frightened him. It was the same with politics. He rarely read more than the headlines in his newspaper these days. He knew of course that the Liberals had won a landslide in the election last years and many changes were planned, but he could not get excited about this anymore. Life in the village went on as it always had and perhaps always would. He did not feel interested in the rest of the world anymore.

With so many thoughts whirling around in his head he found that he was soon across the hill and looking down into his home valley. He stopped again and waited for his thumping heart to slow down. He saw the smoke rising straight up from the cottage chimneys on this still day. John checked his watch. The morning service would be finished. Perhaps he would attend Evensong. It would be comforting to take part in the familiar ritual, but would his sin show on his face and how would he explain to Ebenezer his early return? Perhaps he should go and ask God to forgive him. But who or what was God? Surely he did not believe in all that nonsense. No it would be better to stay at home and try to establish a better relationship with Ella; to be more tolerant and thoughtful towards her and less critical of her faults.

Perhaps this new attitude should also be applied to his step-granddaughter. After all it was not Nan's fault that her short, slim body, her black curls and those bright, dark eyes were a constant reminder of her father or that she had never really been close to John. She worshipped Ella and always took her side. He often caught her looking critically at him when he had sharp words for his wife.

It was not at all surprising that they were so close when one remembered that it was Ella who had discovered five year old Nan sitting beside her dead mother at the edge of Lake Vyrnwy and had immediately taken her into her home and her heart. If it had been his choice the girl would have been put in an orphanage. He wanted nothing to do with this pathetic outcome of a shameful liaison between a devious Welshman and a disobedient step daughter. But Ella was determined to take the child in whatever he said. Now Nan was seventeen and must soon go out into the world. There was no doubt that she was intelligent and determined. Well the sooner she moved on to whatever life she chose the sooner he would be a happier man. But for the moment perhaps he should try to be nicer to Nan as well.

In a day or two he would be back at the school, trying to turn sow's ears into silk purses. No, that wasn't fair either. At least a couple of pupils from each year showed above average intelligence which if fostered might help them to escape the drudgery of agricultural labouring or domestic service. It was simply that he was tired of his profession, of going through yet another year of the same old routine. He could run his school with eyes shut, meet the basic standards the inspectors required, appear to the inhabitants of Hope Underhill to be a skilled and successful headmaster. He was simply weary of it all.

He was glad there was no-one about in the village. When he reached the church he heard the choir practising the hymns for the evening service. He smiled at the irony of hearing, 'Lead kindly light, amid the encircling gloom.' when he was about to face the wife he had wronged.

The school stood next to the church and next to that stood the master's house and there outside the door was hitched a fine stallion. There was only one person in the village who could own such a splendid horse. John's guilt turned at once to jealousy. What was Robert Moreton doing here?

In the early days of his return to Hope Underhill Robert had been his closest friend. Together they had unmasked the wicked rector, who had murdered John's predecessor at the school. The Reverend Whiting, having been rejected by Harriet Owen when he had asked her to be his wife, had subsequently killed her in the barley field. But many men were taken with the beautiful Miss Owen and at first John had even suspected that Robert, who was a young rake at the time, might have been responsible, but once that misunderstanding had been overcome they had worked well together to find the guilty party.

In those days Robert was known throughout the neighbourhood as a heavy drinker, gambler and womaniser. And among the women he pursued was Ella, then a young widow, living with her daughter in a lonely cottage belonging to the Manor. But when his father, Squire Moreton, died, Robert's whole character changed. He gave up his disreputable ways, and settled down to become an efficient, innovative land owner. Meanwhile John and Ella had met, fallen in love and married.

He had known that Robert remained fond of Ella, even though he had a place in a much higher strata of society and considerable responsibility. There was no suspicion of misconduct and it was obvious that Ella loved her husband, but Robert had always taken an interest in young John, their son, helping with his fees at a local public school, and with his expenses when he went on to university. John was very grateful for this help as a headmaster's salary would certainly not have funded the school or the university, but sometimes it made him feel inadequate and occasionally he wondered why the squire should be so generous to another man's son.

Over the years he and Robert had drifted apart. This was partly to do with their difference in social class, but also because they had few shared interests. Robert loved to ride and hunt and shoot, when he was not managing the estate, while John was happier with his books and a quiet walk among the hills.

So what was Moreton doing here now, when John was not expected to return until tomorrow? What was going on?

He did not immediately go to the door, but peered instead through the window and saw Moreton comfortably ensconced in John's own armchair beside the fire, while Ella stood behind it and seemed to be caressing the man's head. Flushed with anger John returned to the door, lifted the latch and burst into the room. Ella drew back abruptly from Moreton's chair.

'Why, John. What are you doing back home today?'

Unabashed Moreton rose and offered John his hand, then lowered it again as he did not respond. John looked from one to the other, his face flushed, his heart beating fast. Ella came towards him and pecked him on the cheek. John steadied his voice as he explained.

'The weather was poor and the hotel uncomfortable, so I decided to come home. What brings you here, Robert?'

'Well, I really came to see young John. I had heard he was coming home today. But when I was riding down to the village, someone's damn dog leapt at my horse, which reared up and threw me off. I was showing your dear wife the bump on the back of my head, which she was about to bathe. Here, look? '

Robert bent down. John saw that indeed there was a large contusion on the back of his head, which looked very painful.

'It's my own fault of course. I was not wearing a helmet, as it was such a short journey.'

Ella looked closely at her husband.

'Are you all right, my dear? You seem quite out of breath. Have you walked all the way from Churchtown? That was foolish. You know how walking tires you these days. Shall I make you some tea?'

John felt very foolish. He tried to make amends.

'No. Deal with Robert's injury first. Then we'll have tea together.

I can't offer you anything stronger, I'm afraid. This is a teetotal house nowadays.'

'Tea will be...'

At that moment the latch clicked and Nan entered. She too was out of breath, her pale cheeks flushed, and her manners forgotten in the midst of some emergency.

'Oh Ella, Ella...'

John was immediately irritated, his recent resolution soon forgotten.

'Nan! Do you not see we have a visitor?'

Nan gathered her breath.

'Oh yes, Good evening Robert. But Grandmother...Mr Noble... a dreadful thing has happened.'

Ella paled and slumped into the nearest chair, fearing some terrible calamity. Nan continued.

'It's Uncle John. He's been arrested. Old Sergeant Oakes is on his way now to tell you. I ran on so that you were prepared.'

'Arrested!' John and Robert exclaimed in unison.

'Yes, he's been taken to the police station in Shrewsbury and put in a cell.'

There was a loud knock on the door. John went to open it. Nan knelt on the floor beside Ella, who placed her hands comfortingly on her granddaughter's shoulders. Robert moved towards Ella, then changed his mind and stepped back.

Oakes entered. He had been a well-built, round faced young man when John had first met him a quarter of a century ago. Now he was almost as wide as he was tall and, when he removed his helmet, completely bald. He stood in the middle of the room, wiping the sweat from his brow, as if about to address the congregation at the local chapel, where he was a lay-reader.

'Mr Noble, Ella...and er, Squire. I 'as some bad news.'

'Nan has told us...' John began.

'All of it?'

Robert asked, 'Why has he been arrested? Was he drunk?'

'Well, that be a part on it...'

John was suddenly very angry, 'What a fool! The times I have warned him!' He paused. 'Part of it?'

'Not the worst part neither,' Oakes went on. 'He hit a man. Hurt him bad. He's in th'infirmary.'

'Nonsense!' Ella cried out, 'Our John would never hit anyone. He's gentle as a lamb!'

'Well, I aint saying he were'nt provoked but...'

'Look,' said Robert, 'My horse is outside. I'll ride at once to Shrewsbury, arrange bail and have the lad home again, so that we can sort this out.'

'Oh, thank you, Robert' said Ella, rising from the chair. 'Wait a moment while I pack him some cake. He'll be hungry in that cell.' Then she burst into tears. 'John, in prison! I can't believe it.'

'He aint in proper prison yet, Mrs Noble. He aint been tried.'

Ella could only mumble incoherently. Nan rose and put an arm around her grandmother. 'Don't worry, Grandmother, Robert will soon sort it out.'

'Yes, he's a good man.'

They both went into the kitchen.

'Drinking and fighting!' said the elder John, 'Well, I never thought. It seems I am doomed to have disobedient children. I'll have a few things to say to the lad when I see him. '

'That isn't fair, John. We don't know how it happened yet.'

'Mm!' was John's response.

Ella returned and handed a small package to Robert, 'Give the poor boy my love.'

Robert put the package in his jacket pocket and stepped outside. They heard the clatter of hooves on the newly surfaced road gradually fade.

'The best thing we can do now is sit down and have a cup of tea,' said Ella, still shaking with shock.' Will you join us Sergeant?'

'No I must be on my way,' he fastened his helmet on again. 'Always places to go and people to see. I'll bid you farewell. Sorry to be the bearer of bad news'

Oakes gave a little bow and left.

John muttered, 'The place he must go to will be the Three Pheasants and the people he has to see will be his fellow drinkers'

Chapter Six

Philip had sat opposite picking at his food, his eyes widening as I told my tale. It was time to rest my tongue and his ears. So we ate in silence until the meal was finished, then retired to the sitting room, to sit at our ease and smoke. At last Philip could wait no longer, so I had to continue my story.

It was the warmest time of the year in New York. The crowded streets, the stink of unwashed humanity and their piles of waste were almost unbearable. One evening I was sitting in the bar with a couple of friends, enjoying a cool beer at the end of an exceptionally hot day, when this stranger entered. He was a tall, well-built man, dressed in a most unusual way, so that he stood out among us workers in our shabby, sober suiting like a flower growing out of a refuse dump. He wore pale coloured pants – trousers to you- a bright shirt, an even brighter necktie, a leather jerkin with a fringe and a wide Stetson hat. His long legs were slightly bowed as he walked over to our table with his second drink in his hand- the first had been downed at the bar- and introduced himself.

'Howdy. Name's Jed. Jed Timpson. Mind if I join you? Seems like you got an empty seat right here.'

His spoke in a sing-song drawl but his words were clearly enunciated, not like the low growl of most New Yorkers. The others with me seemed to take a dislike to the stranger, for whatever reason, and soon excused themselves, but I found his appearance and way of speaking fascinating. Close up I could see that although his clothes were clean they were well used, even threadbare in places. I bought him a drink and asked what he was doing in New York.

'You heard of Buffalo Bill?' he asked

I certainly had. His real name was William Cody, and he had brought his Wild West Show to New York a few years back and people were still talking about it. Apparently the huge cast enacted scenes from life in the Wild West. There were battles with Indians, marksmanship contest, rodeos and many other spectacular scenes.

'Well,' the stranger continued, 'I came East with the show. I used to do trick riding and took part in the big scenes, but then the whole show went over to Europe and I couldn't face crossing that damned ocean, so I stuck here and did a couple of turns in the Music Halls for a while but I had to sell my horse. Couldn't afford the stabling no more.'

He swallowed another whisky, paused, then asked, 'So what are you doing in this hell-hole? '

At that moment I thought about my gruelling, sweaty work, the oppressive atmosphere of summer in the city, my shared room and sleepless nights and I felt his description was about right. Then he started to tell me about the place he had come from; a State called Wyoming, which he said was more than two thousand miles away.

'I miss it like crazy,' he said. 'We got mountains so high-he raised his arms to show how high- and rivers flowing through green pastures. You ride half a day without seeing another guy. The air's so fresh it almost hurts to breathe.'

The more he told me about the Green River Valley, which was his part of that state, the more it sounded like my homeland and the more I longed to go there.

'So what could a man do over there? For a living I mean?'

'Well there's cattle to run for a man good on a horse. There's farmsteads too, for the family man. And up among the hills there's coal and other stuff to be mined.'

That sounded like something I could do. And in a place that sounded more like heaven every minute who would mind working hard.

'Matter of fact,' he went on, 'I'm about done here myself. Money's getting low. Perhaps we could travel together, if you're interested.'

I was indeed.

'So how would we get there?'

'Mostly by rail, if you can afford it. Then the last part by stage coach.'

'When were you thinking of leaving?' I asked.

'Soon as I can. Money's almost gone. The halls are closed now for the summer break. Who wants to sit in a stinkin' theatre in weather like this?'

We arranged to meet at Grand Central Station next morning to begin our mammoth journey. What I didn't realise at the time was we wouldn't be sitting in a comfortable carriage, admiring the landscapes we were travelling through, because Jed was down to his last few dollars and I was about to discover my own misfortune, but my only thoughts as I walked back to my lodgings that sweltering evening were about The Green River valley which I could already picture clearly in my mind.

As I approached my lodgings I saw the O'Malley's sitting together on a small bench outside the door, poor Samuel squashed against one arm by his ever expanding beloved. But both looked very disconsolate and Maeve was wiping away a tear with a filthy handkerchief. As I came nearer it was Samuel who spoke first.

'Oh Mr Morris! A dreadful thing has happened. That ugly Polack has gone. Done a moonlight flit as they say. Not bothered to pay what he owed us. Left the room in a terrible state.'

At first I was actually quite pleased and looked forward to a quiet night ahead, but I realised that I was about to add to their woes when I gave in my own notice. I decided there and then that I should use my own savings to add a little to my rent in compensation for the short notice.

I briefly commiserated with them before climbing the four flights of stairs to my little room, preparing to drop onto my mattress and have an early night, but when I opened the door I was shocked to find that my mattress had been cut open and its innards scattered about the room, but my shock was even greater when I discovered that my hundred dollars in ten dollar notes, which I had carefully sewn into the mattress had been discovered and taken as well. This left me with only the few dollars in my pocket and would necessitate me doing a moonlight flit as well.

Very early next Monday morning I packed my few belongings into a carpet bag, left the house while the O'Malley's were still asleep and met Jed who was already sitting on the steps outside the station. I told him what had happened. He was shocked, but then smiled.

'Seems like we're both in the same boat,' he said.

'So how do we get to Wyoming?'

'On the train.'

'How do we do that without tickets?'

He smiled again.

'Follow me.'

He set off down the street with his long stride, stopped at a store to buy some bread and a chunk of cheese, which he put in his shoulder bag and a couple of beers, which I stuck in my jacket pockets. Soon we turned into a side street. There were drab brownstone houses down one side of this street and on the other side a long, high wall. From over the wall I could hear the occasional clanking of metal on metal and sometimes smoke and steam rose above the wall and dropped sooty smuts down onto us. I thought there must be a furnace or some such on the other side.

We came to a gate in the wall, where wagons were going in and out, after being checked carefully by a gateman in a little hut.

'Do exactly what I do,' Jed whispered.

When the next big wagon turned into the gate he ducked down between the wheels. I did the same, but was worried that when the wagon moved on I would be caught under its huge iron-rimmed rear wheels. The gateman lifted the tarpaulin cover off the goods on his side of the wagon and signalled the driver to move on. We heard him shout at the horses, crack his whip and the wagon rumbled forward. It was really difficult in that cramped position to stumble along at the same pace as the wagon, and my back began to ache from being bent over like that, but after a while we heard the driver shout, 'Whoa!' and the wagon came to a halt. Jed leapt out and ran towards some trucks moving slowly behind a large, dirty locomotive. I followed close behind. He found what looked like a cattle wagon with the side door open, jumped up and got in. I ran along beside the moving train until Jed caught my hands and I realised for the first time just how strong he was as he lifted me almost bodily into the wagon. I lay panting on the wooden floor but soon sat up because the thin layer of straw on that floor stank abominably.

At first I thought the wagon was empty but as my eyes became accustomed to the darkness – Jed had closed the door- I realised that we were not alone. There were a couple of shadowy figures slumped against the wagon walls on the other side.

'Howdy,' said Jed to the other occupants, 'D'you happen to know where we're heading?'

A deep voice spoke out of the darkness.

'East. Got to be East. Otherwise we'd be in the Atlantic by now.'

There was general laughter.

'First stop Philadelphia' said another voice.

I had no idea where Philadelphia was, or what kind of a place it was or how far away it was, but Jed seemed happy about our direction. He spoke softly. 'That's good. Philadelphia is good. I remember coming through it on the way east.'

The thing about America is its size. What we would consider in England or Wales to be a long journey – say Liverpool to London – is just a stroll over there. The truck we were in rattled and bumped slowly along the track for hours and hours and the stink of that filthy straw grew stronger. Gradually the sluggish conversation ceased and we all lay back despite the hardness of the floor and the choking smell of the straw and tried to sleep. I must have dozed off at last because when I woke Jed was shaking my shoulder. Suddenly I realised that we were not moving anymore.

'Where...?' I began but Jed shushed me.

'Get back...' he whispered, 'far as you can. Pull the straw over you.'

I did as he said, sliding back on my backside and pulling the straw over me. Suddenly the door of the car opened, and in the light I saw that the others had already gone. Something banged against the side, men outside began to shout and beat on animal hides with sticks and the animals lowed in panic as they were forced up into the wagon.

'We've got to get out, Jed' I almost shouted, but I wouldn't have been heard in that din.

'No,' he said. 'Not yet. But stand up.'

I did so, just as one of the animals came right up to me and almost squashed me against the side with its heavy flank.

After more shouting and smacking of sticks on animal hides the door was slid shut, the wagon jerked, and moved slowly forward.

'Now,' shouted Jed. He jumped onto the back of one of the beasts. It tried to shake him off but the cattle were so crammed in that they could hardly move.

I started to struggle up onto another animal. I was not as tall or as strong as Jed but I managed it at last. Meanwhile he had reached up and pushed open a hatch in the roof of the wagon. When he was out on the roof he lowered his arms and helped to pull me out as well. Soon I lay flat out on the roof, panting and terrified. The train was moving quite fast by now and I expected to slip off the roof to my death at any moment.

Jed was sitting on the roof, facing forward, with his legs apart as if he was sitting on a very wide horse. The sides of his jacket blew out in the wind and I saw that hanging from his belt there was a holster, containing a revolver and on the opposite side a small tin mug.

I tried to sit in the same way as Jed, but every time I moved I felt myself slipping.

Jed laughed. 'Let me give you a hand' He held on to me while I slowly changed my position until I was sitting like him but facing the rear of the train. I kept glancing nervously backwards, expecting to be decapitated at any moment by a low bridge or a tunnel.

'It's OK,' Jed shouted. 'I'll let you know when we come to a tunnel. There aint none for a while.'

'What happened to the others?'

'They got out at Philly, as they called it. Joining some guy called Coxey on a march to Washington to protest about all the unemployment. You were fast asleep at the time.'

We were passing through the outskirts of a city, where dense smoke rose from many factories and foundries. Soon we came to a bridge over a wide river. As the train rattled across that long iron bridge my fear returned as I looked down at the fast flowing waters far below. Then we were out of the city and heading towards a long mountain ridge.

Jed had managed to hold on to his shoulder bag while he climbed onto the roof. My carpet bag was still in the car and would be trampled to pieces by now. He opened the bag and handed me a squashed hunk of bread and a piece of cheese. I remembered the bottles of beer in my jacket pockets. Incredibly they were still there and unbroken. I took one out and handed it to my companion. He twisted off the top with his teeth and caught the shaken beer as it erupted from the bottle. I followed his example and at last managed to remove the cap. My jaws ached but the beer tasted very good. When we finished the beer we slung the bottles away

The sun was already going down. Jed pointed behind me. I glanced round to see that we were moving into a landscape of wooded hills and beyond that those real mountains loomed purple under the setting sun.

'What do we do now?' I asked.

'Wait awhile. 'Train 'ull slow down soon, 'cause of the gradient. Then we jump off and rest up for a while.'

I looked at the ground rushing by on either side, with thorn bushes and rock sticking out of the thin soil and could not imagine jumping down without breaking every limb.

At last the sun disappeared completely, behind those mountains. The temperature dropped abruptly and we were forced to button up our coats. The train began to slow and the sound of the locomotive echoed loudly as rock walls closed in on either side. The thump, thump of the pistons became more and more pronounced as the train climbed slowly upwards.

'This is where we get off,' Jed shouted.

I looked down at the side of the track. There was grass now, instead of soil and rocks, but it still seemed a long way away. When I looked again at Jed, he had gone. I shuffled to the edge of the roof, leant forward and jumped, rolling over as I hit the ground, and gasping as the air was forced out of my lungs.

I lay on the damp ground, listening to the retreating clatter of the train and checking my limbs for breakages. There were none but several bruises were beginning to throb on my buttocks and shoulders. The train disappeared round a bend and an enormous silence filled the night.

'You gonna lay there for ever?'

I sat up and saw Jed in silhouette against the starry sky.

'This is wild country,' he went on. 'We need to find a sheltered spot and get a fire going. Follow me.'

I struggled to my feet and followed him as he walked into the forest. He seemed to see the way quite clearly, while I stumbled behind him, tripping over tufts of grass and fallen branches. Soon a dark shape reared up ahead and I could hear the sound of rushing water nearby. We came to a clearing in the trees at the bottom of a rocky outcrop. My eyes had become accustomed to the darkness by now and I could see that there was a shallow cave in the rock. Jed stood at the mouth of this short cave and listened, then shouted 'Yowee!' but nothing came out of the darkness.

I wondered what he had expected to find but did not dare to ask.

Jed was already making a small pile of leaves and twigs on the flat ground at the entrance to the cave.

'Gather as much dry stuff as you can and quick'

So I walked back towards the trees and pulled out some thin dead branches. Some of these were brittle enough to be broken into smaller pieces which I carried across to where Jed was kneeling and blowing on the small flame he had started among the tinder. Soon we had a good blaze going. We collected more timber and stacked it at the side of the fire. Jed lifted a burning branch from the fire and took it into the short cave. A small rodent shot out between his legs but that was all.

'Just checking for snakes. There aint none. And they won't come while the fire's going.'

We sat in silence for a while, enjoying the warmth and sense of security that the fire gave us.

'You thirsty?' asked Jed. Of course I was. We'd had nothing to drink since that beer. He unhooked that metal cup from his belt. Then he stood, pulled out another small burning branch from the fire. He beckoned me to follow him. I kept close to him as he walked round the base of the rock and soon we came to a small waterfall tumbling from a cleft in the rock. At the foot of this there was a deep pool.

'Take care. Them rocks is slippery,'

He dipped his cup into the pool, sniffed the water, then drank deeply.

'That's good.'

He filled the cup again and handed it to me. The water was very cold and had a metallic taste but it certainly slaked my thirst. We shared a few more cupfuls then returned to our fire and stuck on some more branches.

'What do we do now?' I asked.

'One of us keeps the fire going while the other sleeps. I'll take first watch. You look about done in.'

I didn't have the strength to argue. I lay down and pulled my jacket round me. I thought it would be hard to sleep in these circumstances but almost as soon as my head touched the ground my eyes closed and I was out for the count.

Chapter Seven

The police officer led Robert to the cells and unlocked the one where young John was lying on a wooden bench. When he sat up Robert saw that he had been crying. He went over to the younger man and sat beside him.

'Hey, there's no need for tears. They've let me pay your bail. We'll soon have you home again.'

'Home! I'm never going home again. The man's a murderer.'

'What man?'

'My father!'

'What d'you mean?'

'The man in the Red Lion told me the truth. I didn't believe him at first. He said something about Amy that made me very angry. That's why I hit him. How is he by the way?'

'Apparently he's much better now. He'll spent the night in the infirmary, under observation, but go home tomorrow. You must have hit him pretty hard.'

'I feel bad about that now. I suppose I'll go to prison.'

'No...No. There'll be a fine at the most. But what's this about your father being a murderer? And what did this man say about Amy? I want you to tell me the whole story. But not in this place. Let's get you out of here and you can tell me everything as we ride home.'

Robert left his horse at the stables and hired a gig. Soon they were riding southwards and John began his tale.

'I was travelling back from Wiltshire, after staying at my friend's estate near Salisbury. It was quite warm for the time of year and by the time the train reached Shrewsbury I was very thirsty. As you know my father won't allow alcohol in the house but I find a pint or two of good ale very satisfying, especially on a hot day. I don't use the village pub because he would get to hear of it, but there are plenty of hostelries nearby where I am not so well known.'

'I suppose I should have had something to eat but my thirst was great and after a few pints I began to feel rather drunk. Then this man asked if he could join me and I let him buy me another pint. I didn't recognise the man. I suppose he was in his late thirties, but looked much older, very wiry, with a tanned, weather-beaten face.'

'He told me that he had lived in our village as a boy and had gone to the village school. He called my father a cruel tyrant who had taken a particular dislike to him and caned him frequently. He could still remember the swish of that cane as it cut into his hand.'

'I was not particularly disturbed by this. After all we know that my father can be very strict, though I did not like to hear that he hated one boy more than the others, but then this man, Richard his name was...Richard Belkins I think he said.'

Robert interrupted, 'Oh that Belkins. A notorious family. Poachers and petty thieves all. Mind you it's the father I know best, in my role as magistrate. I seem to remember that Richard, the youngest boy, left home as soon as he could.'

'Yes well, Richard told me why my father hated him so much. It was to do with my half-sister, Amy. Apparently Richard was besotted with her. All the older boys were, but Richard decided that he would let her know how he felt about her. One day at the end of school he asked Amy to help him. Said he was having trouble with his arithmetic. Well of course she agreed. You know what Amy was like. They went together into a quiet corner of the playground and he showed her something, but it wasn't his maths book. She screamed and ran towards the classroom, which her stepfather was just leaving. He asked Amy what was the matter. She didn't snitch but the master saw Richard skulking near the hedge and put two and two together. He took him back into the school and caned him viciously without even asking him what had happened.'

'Then this Richard said something that made me want to hit him, but I managed to restrain myself. He said, "Reckon your old man fancied her himself". I knew he was just being provocative. Obviously he hated my father so much.'

'He told me how he had left the village as soon as possible and gone to sea. He got flogged a couple of times but mostly he liked being aboard ship. He'd seen a good bit of the world and had a girl in many a port. He'd gone back to the village now and then, to see his mother. Made sure that his father was away, as he often was, usually in jail. Caught up with all the village news. Kept an eye on my father and watched me growing up. He had made enquiries about us and that's how he discovered that Amy was dead. Of course he was shocked, he said, but not really surprised.'

'The way he said that puzzled me. I asked what he meant.'

"Well, you see, Liverpool was a port where we often landed. I was second mate by then and the last trip had left me with money in my pocket. I decided to live like a lord while it lasted so I booked into a good hotel, ate and drank well, then looked about for some entertainment. I soon had this little doxy by my side – I reckon they can smell money- and was about to take her up to my room when this party of toffs come in, with a couple of women. I recognised her at once. Amy I mean. Even though she were dressed like a lady and her face was made up, I knew her at once and knew what she had become."

'I don't understand, I said...'

"Neither did I, but I made some discreet enquiries and discovered it was your bloody father's fault. Poor Amy, your lovely sister, had got pregnant, but when she told your father he turned her out of the home, the bastard, and she was forced to go right away and make a living for herself and her little girl. And that's what she'd done. High class of course, but still a whore..."

'That's when I hit him. Took him by surprise and he just sat there with his mouth open. So I hit him again, knocking him to the floor and would have gone on hitting him but thankfully the landlord came across and held me, while someone went for the police...'

'You believed this man?'

'Not at first, but then it began to make sense. Poor, poor Amy, and all because my father turned her away when she most needed help. That's why I'll never go home while he is there.'

'What will you do?'

'Strangely enough someone has made me an offer that exactly fits the bill.'

'Which is?

'When I was staying at my friend's house they had a visitor. A man well known as an explorer. He had travelled to the Antarctic with Ernest Shackleton on his last expedition and had had the most amazing adventures. He and I hit it off straight away and he suggested that I join the next expedition which is setting off later this year. I told him that I was just about to begin my final year at university, but he said that the experience would count for much more. Of course I would only be a junior member of the team -sort of dogsbody- but my scientific studies would be useful.'

'What did you say to him?'

'That I would think about it. But now of course it seems to be the ideal solution.'

'So you will give up your studies?'

'Look Uncle Robert – you don't mind me calling you that do you? – you have helped me so much, first with my schooling and then with going on to university. I am very grateful for that. Indeed I will be for ever in your debt. But this is an opportunity not to be missed. And not simply to get away from my father. It will be a life changing experience. And I promise that I shall make you proud of me.'

'Do you really have to go the ends of the earth to avoid your father?'

'Of course not, but can you imagine what it will be like. I have since read something about the place. The great sheets of ice, several miles thick in places. Those funny flightless birds called penguins and the enormous whales that live in that southern ocean.'

'What of the intense cold?'

'I'm sure we'll be equipped to deal with that.'

'Speaking of clothes. Do you have enough to manage for the moment? In your luggage I mean.'

'No, I suppose...'

'I have an idea. Come back with me to the Manor. I'll contact your mother. She can bring what you need. And you can say farewell properly to her.'

When Ella arrived at the Manor she was in tears. Nan had accompanied her. She was not crying but her eyes were bright with excitement.

'Oh, Uncle John, how exciting. To go with that great man to the South Pole...'

'Well, I don't think we will actually be making for the pole this time. It's more of a scientific expedition.'

Ella hugged her son. 'Do you really have to go? Couldn't you talk to your father? Try to make peace with him.'

'That's not possible, mother. After what I've heard.'

Nan looked puzzled, 'Heard what?'

John realized immediately that he had said too much. It would hurt Nan deeply if he tried to explain. Ella continued.

'We all make mistakes John. I'm sure that your father regrets his actions now.'

The brightness in Nan's eyes faded. Her face twisted with anxiety.

'What's this all about?'

It was Robert who came to the rescue.

'Nan dear, I think we should let your grandmother have some time alone with her son. And I have something to show you.'

Nan was reluctant to leave but eventually she shrugged and left the room with Robert, but as soon as they entered the next room, they found a servant waiting. He approached his master.

'What is it Frederick?'

Message from the stables, Sir. There's been an incident. You're to come at once.'

'Is it that urgent?'

'Yes, Sir, I'm afraid it is.'

'Shall I come with you?' asked Nan.

'No, you wait here, my dear. I'll be back as soon as I can.'

At first Nan walked around the room, studying the dreary portraits of Robert's ancestors, but hearing raised voices she moved back towards the closed door and listened.

'How could he have turned your daughter away like that? When she most needed your help. With that baby inside her. Why didn't you stop him?'

'Because I was weak and foolish, and a little afraid of him at that time. I thought he would soon change his mind. That Amy would come back and all would be well. Your father is not a wicked man.'

'I beg to differ. There is no excuse for what he did. Amy was forced into prostitution. Then she became ill with some horrible disease associated with that profession.'

Ella began to sob loudly. 'I know, I know. But she had to give little Nan a decent life.'

'Hardly decent, Mother. Does Nan know nothing of this?'

'No, and you must never...'

Nan flung open the door. Her face was crimson with anger

'I have every right to know...everything...and I want to know now.'

'But why, dear Nan? Haven't you been happy with me? I gave you all the love I could.'

'Oh, Granny, of course I have been happy with you. You have always been kind to me. And Uncle John as well. But I have always felt that Mr Noble resented me. I could never call him Grandfather. It was the way he looked at me.'

'I suppose...'began Ella, but she could not find excuses for her husband.

'John, I heard you say that my mother had become a prostitute. Was that true?'

'Yes'

Ella said, 'Surely Nan, you don't even know what that is.'

'It's no good mother. Nan needs to know. We must face facts. You see, Nan, it was for your sake. She was expecting you. She was homeless. She had no means of support. In the eyes of the world she was already a fallen woman. She could see no other way.'

'But she had a home. Here in Hope Underhill. She had a loving mother and a stepfather who could easily have supported her.'

'Well...'began Robert, but Ella interrupted.

'No, I will tell her Robert, because I was the most to blame. You see, when Amy told us that she was pregnant John said that she must go and find the father and make him marry her. He could not bear the thought that as a respected member of the community he would have to live with the shame of harbouring a sinful woman and her bastard child. And he thought he might even be asked to resign as the master of a church school.'

'And you let him do this?'

'Oh, Nan, you cannot know how often I have regretted it. Every day the guilt has tortured me. But you see I really thought that when John had cooled down he would get in touch with Amy and tell her to come home and when he saw the baby – you- he would change his mind. But by this time Amy had disappeared. I had no idea where to look for her. And we did not know at that time that your father was in prison.'

'In prison!'

'Yes, wrongly accused of criminal damage. And the only person who could have given him an alibi had vanished.'

John intervened. 'The man who told me about your mother seemed to think that at that time she was living in rather a grand house in Liverpool run by a woman of considerable means.'

Nan paused in silent thought.

'Ye...s, I do remember that when I was very small we had a lovely room in a house full of women and that my mother always wore fine clothes.'

'Then I suppose Amy got ill and was no use to this woman anymore. So she threw her out. Just as her stepfather had.'

'Well,' said Nan, 'I won't wait to be thrown out. I shall simply leave.'

'Oh no,' said Ella, 'Please, no! Not you as well?'

'I'm sorry, Grandmother, but I could never live in the same house as that man, now I know what he did.'

'But what will you do?' asked John.

'I will come with you, if you will let me. I have some savings. I will find a room in Shrewsbury and get work as soon as I can.'

'Nan, Oh Nan. I shall miss you so much.'

'Don't worry. I will visit regularly whenever Mr Noble is out of the way. And once I am settled you can visit me.'

Ella smiled, then had a thought, 'Look, at the moment Mr Noble has gone to bed. He was worn out after the journey. He will be asleep for some time. Ask Robert to lend you a carriage. We can load it with some of your things, Nan. Then you can both be on your way before he wakes up.'

At that moment Robert returned. He saw Ella being hugged by her son and granddaughter and smiled.

'Well, well, you seem to have sorted everything out.'

'What was the emergency?' asked Nan.

'Nothing really. The new stable boy was worried about one of the horses. Thought it might be lame. Still it shows how conscientious he is. He'll do well with more experience.'

'And what did you want to show me?'

'I'm afraid that was just a ruse'

Nan smiled. John said, 'Uncle Robert, I have a favour to ask'

Of course, Robert soon agreed and in a short while the two youngsters set off, in the gig that Robert had already hired and which they would return to the stables when they reached Shrewsbury; one taking the first step of a momentous journey, the other simply a step into the unknown. Ella kept her tears at bay until the gig had disappeared over the hill towards Shrewsbury. For a moment she almost decided to follow them, but knew she would never have that sort of courage. Now she let the tears flow as she contemplated her future, trapped for the rest of her life in a relationship with a man she now despised.

Chapter Eight

It was early evening by the time Nan and John had returned the gig, left their luggage at the railway station and made their way across the footbridge which crossed the lines and connected the station with that area of Shrewsbury just to the north of the old castle and appropriately called Castlefields. At the end of the footbridge they turned right, going past the impressive gatehouse of Shrewsbury Gaol with the statue of John Howard, the great prison reformer, set in a niche above the door. John shuddered at the thought that he too might soon have been passing through that door if he had not had Robert's help.

The street ran alongside the prison wall, sloping down towards the river. At the bottom the houses began and they consulted the first of a list of addresses they had copied from the latest edition of the Chronicle. When they reached it the first house looked very suitable, a three storey terrace with clean brickwork and shining windows which on the other side of the house would overlook the River Severn.

John rang the bell and a middle-aged woman came to the door. She was tall and thin, dressed all in black, with a face that suggested permanent mourning. John explained that they were looking for a room for his sister. The woman drew in her breath sharply, saying, 'Em afraid we do not take in single ladies. The area has a bad enough reputation as it is.' She withdrew and closed the door before John could say another word.

That 'reputation' seemed to be confirmed when they called at another, less impressive dwelling in the next street. As John reached for the bell the door swung open and a couple of, possibly, youngish women- it was difficult to tell their ages under all that rouge and lipstick- rushed out, giggling and sauntered up the street, arm in arm. They were in common parlance 'ladies of the town'. John returned to the bell, which sounded somewhere within and eventually a large woman, carelessly dressed and with her greying hair unsuccessfully dyed a sort of crimson came out and looked apprais-ingly at Nan, while John explained what they needed. She continued to stare at Nan and some kind of light ignited in her sunken eyes, then she smiled, saying, 'Well we do 'ave a little room at the top. I'm sure it would suit the young lady. Do come in.'

John was about to answer when he felt Nan's hand pulling at his sleeve and he bent down to hear her whisper something. John cleared his throat and said, 'My sister thinks the house is too close to the river. She suffers dreadfully from her chest.'

The woman looked disappointed. 'Please yourself!' she said and closed the door. Nan led John smartly away from the house, explaining, 'There was just something about that woman. The way she looked at me. It made my flesh creep.'

After two more refusals in the next street, and with the awareness that night was closing in, they stopped to reconsider their plan. Suddenly John had an idea.

'That gold ring, with the small stone, will it fit the third finger on your left hand?'

Nan was puzzled but tried it and it did indeed fit.

'Now turn it round so that you cannot see the stone'

Nan was even more puzzled now, but again she did as she was told.

'Now, when I try the next house, just agree with everything I say.'

'Very well, but...'

John studied that list, then led Nan forward into the next street, where he knocked on the shining door of a well-kept house.

A man came to the door, still chewing something from his evening meal.

'Yes'

'I'm sorry to call so late,' began John, 'but I believe you have a room to let.'

'That's the wife's business' he said, then called, 'Agnes. Young couple as wants that room.'

Nan blushed as she saw John's plan. She checked that the ring was still the right way round.

When Agnes appeared, Nan knew at once that she liked her. She was only a few years older and had a warm smile. She shook John's hand and introduced herself.

'I'm Agnes. Agnes Burton. You've met my husband. You wanted to see the room?' She looked at them again. 'It's quite small you know.'

'Ah,' said John, 'Let me explain. The room is really only for my wife. We've just got married and then, well, I've been posted abroad. I'm with the regiment you see. So I wanted somewhere safe for her to stay until she can join me. If we like the room I'll fetch her things and then get back to the barracks.'

They followed the landlady up to a room on the second floor, quite small as she had said, but clean and pleasantly furnished. There was a three quarter bed, with a colourful quilt, a single wardrobe, a table and chair under the window, which had a view of a long back garden.

'Oh, John,' said Nan. 'It's perfect. I'm sure I'll be quite happy here. Until you send for me.'

'Very well. Now Mrs Burton, I'll pay for a few weeks rent and board in advance and the rest...'

'That's fine Mr...er...'

He stood to attention and almost saluted. 'Captain Brown, at your service Ma'm.'

He handed over some money to Mrs Burton, then put a few pounds in Nan's hand as well.

'Now I must fetch your luggage, Mary dear.'

Nan was momentarily non-plussed, then understood. Very well, she was to be Mary Brown for the moment, so that if her step-Grandfather started to look for her, he would be thrown off the scent. Mind you, she couldn't imagine him bothering. Probably pleased to be rid of her.

'Look Mary, I haven't put the things away from our evening meal. Can I offer you a little bread and cheese? I make my own pickles.'

Nan's mouth began to water. She had a healthy appetite and hadn't eaten for ages.

'That would be lovely, Mrs Burton.'

'Oh, call me Agnes. I'm sure we're going to be good friends.'

They followed John down the stairs. Nan kissed him on the cheek as a good wife should, then turned to follow Agnes, into the dining room.

Chapter Nine

It was still dark when I woke again. Jed had just put some more wood on the fire so that it flared up.

'You OK?' he asked.

'Yep,' I said, unconsciously copying Jed's manner of speaking. He settled on the ground, whispered, 'night' and was soon snoring gently. I did not mind his snoring. It was not like that Polack's thunderous droning, and after all I was meant to stay awake. The night was very cold. The stars above burned fiercely. I moved closer to the fire. For almost the first time since I had arrived in America I began to think back over the last few years of my life. First I thought about Amy and me trapped in that tower beside the lake while the water rose towards us. I thought about our lovemaking. I wondered what had happened to her since. Perhaps she was teaching somewhere now or had got married and had children. I hoped she was happy. Then I thought of Nan, my dear younger sister. I didn't know then that her name had been passed on to another young girl, but I reckoned it was a suitable tribute. Where had my sister gone? Why did she not try to contact me when I was shut up in that jail? I saw Ty Craig, not as I had last seen it, shuttered up and beginning to decay, but as it was when my mother and father were alive and we were surrounded by the animals on our little farm.

I rose to fetch some more firewood and tried to break away from those memories. I knew that the only way for me now was to go forward, in this vast new land, to whatever waited for me in the west.

At last the black night thinned and I was able to distinguish earth from sky, then gradually grass from trees. Jed woke and sat up. I was about to speak, when he put a finger to his lips and drew his revolver. I thought someone must be on our trail, but why would there be? Suddenly I saw the flash from the barrel of his gun and a shot rang out. I dropped to the ground, expecting someone to fire back, but Jed just laughed.

'Just got us some breakfast, Huw.'

He walked towards the trees and came back with a rabbit. He took out a small knife from its sheath, also hanging from his belt, slit the rabbit's corpse, removed some of its innards, then drew off its skin. I had seen Mam do this many a time, but what he did next was new to me. He went to the little pool by the waterfall, took mud from the edge and coated the rabbit with it. Then he returned to the fire and dropped the rabbit into the hot ashes.

'Ok, so now we got time to get clean while our breakfast cooks.'

He began to strip off his clothes before walking to that pool and immersing himself in the freezing water. I laughed, remembering an occasion when I had similarly stripped and swam in that lake on the Welsh mountain called Cadair Idris. Philip had stolen my clothes, for a joke. I remembered Amy studying my naked body before turning away as if she had not noticed. I had been embarrassed but excited at the same time.

Now the sun was up and the air was warming rapidly, so I joined Jed in the pool. After all these were the only clothes I had so I needed to keep my body clean. When he got out and the surface of the water stilled I saw a reflection of my face with a dark fuzz of whiskers and wondered when I would next be able to shave.

Soon Jed lifted the rabbit out of the fire and broke away its covering which had hardened like fired pottery. Oh, how good that meat was and with some clear water from the fall to swill it down, I hadn't enjoyed a meal so much for a long time.

I asked Jed how he came to have all this stuff, like that gun and his knife, and where he had learned all the things he knew.

'Well,' he said, 'When you're out on the range driving the cattle, sometimes for days on end, and there aint no store or saloon for fifty miles, you have to fend for yourself. You learn or you die.'

I nodded with understanding and was so glad I had chosen such a companion.

'Ok, time to get on'

'Where do we go? Back to the railroad?'

'No, it's much easier getting off a train than getting on, even if it aint moving too fast. We need to get to a town.'

'So which way do we go?'

'We follow that track.' He pointed to the edge of the trees. 'Reckon I heard some folks using axes just a while ago.'

I could not see a track and I hadn't heard any axes, but I trusted Jed and followed him. And of course he was right, there was a narrow pathway through the trees, which led us up into the hills and soon I heard it too; the thud of axes biting into tree trunks.

We came to a clearing, where about a dozen men were felling trees and stripping them of branches. There were half a dozen powerful looking horses tethered nearby and, when one of the trunks was ready, they were used to drag them away into the forest.

Jed watched the men for a while, then walked over to a tall, well- built man, who seemed to be supervising the work. They spoke for a while, before Jed returned to me.

'Reckon you can handle an axe?'

Of course I could. You don't live up in the mountains of Wales without learning to do that.

'Yes. Why?'

'Cause, Mr Houston, he's the boss, says if we give him a hand for the rest of the day he'll give us a lift into some town or other – I can't remember the name- in his wagon when he goes home.'

So we set to work, and for once I was better at the task than Jed, but he soon improved. We had to cut the branches from the sides of a fallen trunk. The other men were suspicious of us at first and spoke in an accent which I found difficult to understand – German perhaps or Dutch – but when we stopped for a break they could see we had nothing to eat and it wasn't long before odd scraps of bread and small chunks of cheese were thrown across to us.

By the time Mr Houston called a halt that evening my shoulders and arms felt like they would never move easily again and my hands were covered in blisters. Jed collapsed to the ground with a groan, but struggled back to his feet when one of the horses was harnessed to the wagon and soon we were rumbling down the track behind the other horses dragging the last of the huge trunks. We reached a larger clearing where logs were being lifted by crane onto flat trucks standing on a single track railway siding. Jed lifted his thumb to me and nodded.

At last we reached a small town – just a single street really- with the forest close all round, but it had a saloon, a store and a church, all built of wood.

Mr Houston shook our hands – I rather wished he hadn't as it set my blisters stinging again- and gave us each a couple of dollars.

After eating all we could for our dollars we made our way back to that siding where the logs were being loaded onto trucks. When night fell, and the workers went home, Jed picked the padlock on the little hut they used when there were no logs to load. The stove was still warm and there were coats hanging behind the door. We slept well that night and rose early next morning, filled a couple of bottles with water from a barrel, fixed the padlock back on, climbed up onto one of the trucks and made ourselves comfortable in the gap between two huge tree trunks. As the sun rose we heard a locomotive approaching. The trucks jerked as they were attached to the loco and soon we were moving slowly forward. Before long we joined the main track and picked up speed.

We couldn't be seen in our hiding place, but occasionally one of us would peep out to see where we were. When it was my turn I saw that we were through the mountains and in the middle of another large town, where black smoke billowed up from a line of furnaces. We crossed not one but two wide rivers which split the town into three parts, with several bridges joining those parts. I ducked down as we passed slowly through a station but just managed to read the name 'Pittsburgh' on the station wall. When I told Jed what I'd seen he said that was OK, we were heading in the right direction.

When we were through that town or city the train picked up speed again. All day we lay in our hiding place, bumped and jolted as the train moved steadily along the track, sweating as the sun rose in the sky, almost drugged by the smell of the sun baked timber, wishing we had brought more than one bottle of water each, but at last the sun began to go down and the train jangled over a series of points and came to a halt. We stayed in our hiding place until it was dark, then we both rose and looked around.

What we saw amazed us. We were in the middle of a huge freight depot, with dozens of tracks, and warehouses everywhere. Beyond this depot we could see the lights of a large city, some twinkling like stars from immensely high buildings, taller even than those in New York.

Suddenly a light came on nearby and our truck began to move forward. We jumped down quickly and started to walk towards the city, when a voice behind us called out, 'Hey you! What you doing?

We ran. We heard more shouts and then the barking of dogs. This was serious. By the time we reached the perimeter wall the dogs were close. Jed leapt up and grasped the top of the wall.

'Shit!' he said. 'Glass!'

He took off his jacket and threw it onto the wall, then clambered up again. When he was sitting on top he took my hands and pulled me up to join him. Then we leapt down onto the street, just as those dogs reached the foot of the wall, and ran until we could run no more. Jed stood, panting, holding up his cut hand. I removed his neckerchief, wrapped it round his hand, and pulled it tight. When I looked around again I realised that the streets had come to an end and that across a wide road was a large expanse of black water.

'I know this place,' said Jed. 'Chicago. We did a few shows here on our way east. It's a big city. There's a harbour too.'

I was puzzled and asked, 'You mean we've crossed right over to the Pacific coast.'

'Oh no. It aint on the coast. Just a lake. But a huge one. Bigger than some seas. One of the Great lakes. Lake Michigan.'

'So how much further to Wyoming?'

'Well, I reckon we're about half way. But the rest of the way will be hard. It's mostly open country from here. So I think we ought to find some work someplace so that we can eat and get ourselves a few supplies before moving on. Also we gotta take care. When I was last in this city, I saw the police picking up vagrants and putting them in jail'

'We need a place to rest up and to deal with your hand.'

'It aint so bad. Stopped bleeding now. And reckon I know a place where we can stay. Just got to work out where we are first.'

Jed went back to the end of the street and read the sign.

'OK. We go this way.'

As we walked along Jed told me a bit about Chicago.

'They call it the windy city 'cause of the cold wind that comes down from the north in the winter. About twenty years ago most of the place got burned down in a great fire. It was all built of wood then. Now it's all been rebuilt, but this time with steel and stone. There's some really tall buildings. Wait till you see 'em in daylight. They call them skyscrapers and I reckon that's a damn good name for'm.'

Jed stopped and checked another street sign.

'This is it. 'Bout half way down this street.'

At last he turned into a doorway and we climbed several flights of stairs. Then Jed knocked on a door. A woman's voice spoke from inside.

'Who is it?'

'It's Jed, Cindy. Jed Burrows. Can you let us in?'

'Us?'

'I'm with a mate of mine. He's a good guy.'

Cindy opened the door slowly, still a little suspicious, but when she saw Jed she opened the door wider.

'Well, Jed. It really is you. Come in. Hey what happened?'

She had seen his bandaged hand.

'Oh, it aint nothing, Cindy. This is Huw. He's all the way from England.'

'Wales, actually,' I said, being stupidly pedantic as Julia would have called it.

'Hi Huw.' she said, shaking my hand. 'Any friend of Jed's a friend of mine. But what happened? You both look done in.'

'Later,' said Jed. 'We just need a place to rest up for a while.'

Cindy ushered me to a small sofa, then took Jed off to deal with his hand. When they returned, with his hand neatly dressed, I got a chance to really look at Cindy for the first time. She was a pretty young woman and even in an old housecoat you could see she had a splendid figure.

She pointed to the sofa and Jed sat down beside me, while she disappeared into another room, but soon returned with a bottle of whiskey and three glasses. She poured us both generous measures, then took a minute amount herself and sat on an armchair opposite.

'OK. Now let's hear it.'

So Jed told her our story so far. Then he explained to me that Cindy had worked with him in the Wild West Show. They had done a knife throwing act together. They had become good friends, then a little more than that, and Jed had moved in with her, until the show went on to New York.

Cindy found some bread and meatloaf. It was obvious how tired we were, so she suggested I sleep on the sofa. Jed would have to use the floor, being too long for the sofa but she found some blankets to make the floor softer for him. Cindy wished us good night and went to her room and soon after that I fell asleep.

Chapter Ten

When she woke next morning Nan felt at first rather lonely and apprehensive. She knew that she would miss her grandmother very much, but once the new term had begun her stepfather would be busy in the classroom so she would be able to visit her, secretly, and try to persuade Ella to come to Shrewsbury occasionally, though she knew how Ella hated to leave the village. Now her priority must be to find some employment, after all John's money would not last very long. She wondered where John had managed to get this money, but assumed that Robert was helping again. Oh, how clever and helpful John had been. She would miss him too, especially when he was going so far away. She had made him promise to write as often as possible, but wondered how letters got posted from Antarctica.

She had forgotten to pack a dressing gown so she put on her coat and went down to the bathroom that Agnes had pointed out on the first floor. These houses were quite new and had several modern amenities that were still almost unknown in the village, even at the schoolmaster's house.

After dressing Nan went down to the ground floor and knocked nervously on the kitchen door. But Agnes called a cheerful, 'Come in' and Nan relaxed immediately. Agnes was busy at the sink.

'Good morning, Mary. Would you like a proper breakfast or just tea and toast? David, that's my husband, has already left. He works at the Sorting Office, which is nearby. They start very early in the morning.'

As Agnes brought the toast to the kitchen table, apparently they only used the dining room for main meals, Nan asked.

'You don't have children?'

'Oh no, we've not long been married – two years back- and we want to put a few savings together before we start a family. That's why we decided to let the room. I'm so glad you came along.

I was dreading some old man wanting the room, or a stuck up woman. We'll get on fine.'

Agnes poured tea for both of them and sat at the table.

'What will you do while your husband's away, Mary?'

'I was thinking of doing some charitable work. I thought I'd start looking for something this morning.'

'Good idea. Strike while the iron's hot as they say. More toast?'

Nan re-crossed the station footbridge and came out onto Castle Hill. It was a new experience after the village to see so many people in the street at mid-morning and they all seemed so busy with their errands. It was market day and many of the men were farmers, striding about between sales or purchases at the local Smithfield. Most of them looked rather incongruous in their best clothes and some had already visited the local hostelries which opened early on market days so their faces were flushed and their voices loud. The wives were sober and more business-like as they hurried to buy or order what they would need to last them through the week, before they were whisked back to their farms in carts or carriages according to their status.

But it wasn't only carriages and carts which filled the streets these days. The automobile had begun to appear. Soon the horse would be seen as a means of recreation, to hunt the fox or jump the hurdles of a steeplechase, while the motor car was the way to travel in comfort and style.

Nan reached the top of Castle Hill and stood looking down Pride Hill on the other side. This was the busiest of all Shrewsbury's streets and especially on market day the crowds and the traffic mingled dangerously between the shops on either side. She stood on the spot where an ancient cross had once stood, the site of important meetings, the starting point of many processions and the place where the Welsh rebel, David, the brother of Prince Llewellyn had been hanged, drawn and quartered. But Nan knew nothing of this history and was simply trying to decide where to go next. She needed employment, voluntary work was no use to her. As a country girl, she had many skills, but no training relevant for life in town. She was well educated in comparison with many girls of her age, having stayed at school for the full term and worked very hard, under her step-grandfather's direction, but this education had not equipped her to be a waitress, or a shop assistant or whatever other occupation might be available in the town.

To give her time to think she turned away from the melee at the top of Pride Hill and walked into the comparative peace of St Mary's Street, where fine trees surrounded the little churchyard and the clock chimed the half hour at ten-thirty. But the peace did not last long. Just as Nan started to cross the street to walk in the shade of those trees a huge motor car came hurtling towards her, with black smoke billowing from its exhaust. The driver did not look quite human in a large coat with its collar turned up, a cap pulled down over his forehead and dirty goggles, which made his eyes look like black holes. Nan stepped back onto the pavement as the car accelerated towards her, while the driver squeezed the horn to clear the way before him.

Suddenly a child, a boy of nine or ten, ran out of the church yard gate and into the side of the motor car, which knocked him backwards and ran over his leg. The driver did not appear to see the boy at all and drove on round the bend and down Castle Hill.

The boy lay motionless on the dusty street. A man came running behind him out of the churchyard. He may well have been giving chase. Nan walked over to the boy, knelt beside him, took hold of his wrist and checked his pulse. He was still alive, but obviously unconscious. She looked up at the man who stood gawping at the scene. 'He were stealing...'

'Get help! Quickly!' shouted Nan.

That seemed to bring the man to his senses.

'The Infirmary! It's just back there.' He pointed beyond the church. Shall I carry him?'

'No,' she replied with complete certainty. 'He must not be moved.'

The man nodded and ran off towards the infirmary.

Nan looked back at the boy. He was dirty, his clothes were ragged and he was painfully thin. On the road beside him were two pennies. She quickly put them in the pocket of her skirt.

A small crowd gathered, including a policeman. He directed any traffic around Nan and the boy.

'We ough'ta get him off the road, Miss.'

'No! He must not be moved. Help is on its way.'

She spoke with such certainly that the officer demurred.

Suddenly the boy woke and screamed with pain. Nan took the boy's hand and whispered, 'Where does it hurt?'

The boy looked at her and seemed to calm immediately.

'My leg! It's my f.....g leg!' He squeezed her hand so hard that it was painful. When she looked down it was obvious that the leg was bent at an unnatural angle. Nan took a handkerchief from her pocket and began to wipe the sweat and dirt from his face, saying softly, 'Be brave. Help is on its way.'

At that moment two men came running from the direction of the Infirmary, carrying a stretcher between them, and a plump woman in uniform with grey hair under a nurse's cap was trying to keep up. She was still panting when she spoke to Nan.

'What...happened?'

'He ran into the street. Straight into a motor car. He seemed to bounce off it, but his leg went under the rear wheel. I think that's broken.'

The nurse looked down at the leg and nodded.

'Any other injuries?'

'I don't know. I didn't move him.'

'Good girl.'

The nurse knelt beside the boy, cradled his head in her hands, and lifted it off the road.

'Does that hurt?'

The boy shook his head slightly. She placed her hand on his chest, then his stomach 'Here?' Another slight shake of the head. 'Or here?' Then the boy gasped with pain, 'It's just my bloody leg!'

The nurse beckoned to the men with the stretcher. They came forward and laid it on the ground beside the boy. He held out his hand to Nan and she took hold of it as the men gently eased him onto the stretcher. He cried out as they lifted his shattered leg. They lifted the stretcher and prepared to move off.

'Lucky you had your accident so near the infirmary,' said the nurse, then she turned to Nan, who still had the boy's hand in hers. 'Thank you very much for your help, dear. You did well. But we can manage now.'

'No, please,' the boy pleaded, 'Come with me. Please.'

Nan tried to remove her hand, but the boy grasped it more tightly.

'Please!'

'Oh well, 'said the nurse. 'We'd better humour him. At least until he's been seen by the surgeon.'

So the little procession moved forward. The nurse led the way, followed by the men carrying the stretcher and with Nan walking beside them, still holding the boy's hand. He winced with pain at each slight jolt, but smiled back at Nan when she smiled and told him he was being very brave.

They hadn't far to go. The Infirmary was an impressive stone building just behind the church, with wide steps leading up to a pillared portico and the title Salop Infirmary set in the stonework above the doorway. The procession did not enter through this doorway, but made its way instead to a door at the side of the building and into a tiled corridor. A line of chairs had been placed on one side of this corridor, mostly occupied with patients waiting to be seen. But the nurse led them past this glum looking queue and into a small room, where the men placed the stretcher on a leather-covered table, then left the room.

The boy's eyes were closed but he continued to grip Nan's hand. The nurse went away for a moment and returned with a large red-faced man wearing an apron over his suit. He looked at the boy, then stroked his bushy moustache, and muttered, 'Soon have that sorted out. Would you move aside young lady.'

The boy's grip tightened again and he moaned loudly. There was panic in the sound this time.

'He insists on having her nearby, Sir,' said the nurse.

'Relative are you?' enquired the man.

'Oh no,' replied Nan. 'I just happened to be there when the boy was knocked over.'

'And very well she did, Sir,' the nurse added.

'I see.' He walked across the room and lifted a handbell. As it rang the two men reappeared and stood waiting for instructions.

The man – Nan presumed he was a doctor – whispered to the nurse and she left the room, briefly, returning with a dish, giving off a strange sweet smell.

The doctor lifted a cloth from the dish and spoke to the boy.

'Relax now. I'm just going to wash your face with some disinfectant. It's got a funny smell but it will remove any germs.'

'But it aint my face what 'urts...'began the boy but soon he was asleep and his grip on Nan's hand relaxed.

The doctor gave the men some instructions and they lifted the stretcher and took the boy away, followed by the doctor.

'Well,' said the nurse to Nan, 'I think we deserve a cup of tea after that. Come along.'

She led the way into an even smaller room next door, where there were two armchairs and a scrubbed table laid out with a teapot, cups, and a jug of milk. The nurse lifted a kettle onto a gas ring and ushered Nan to one of the chairs. She made tea, passed a cup to Nan, and sat down in the other chair.

'I'm Sister Morgan,' she said. 'You are?'

In all the recent excitement Nan almost forgot, but remembered just in time, 'Mary...Mary Brown.'

'Well Mary, you certainly have an aptitude for nursing. How old are you?'

Nan added a year to her age, 'Eighteen.'

'Had you thought of nursing for a career?'

'Yes, I think I would like to be a nurse. How do I begin?'

'Well, we have a new group of probationers starting soon. The salary is very low, but your needs will be provided for at the Nurses Home. In the meantime, why don't you come in as a volunteer? Many girls begin the training and find after a short while that they are not suited or that we do not find them suitable.'

'I would like that very much.'

'Very well, I will arrange for you to meet the matron. I am sure she will be pleased to have, especially with my recommendation. Of course we will require references.'

Nan nodded as if that would be no problem.

'Have you finished your tea?'

Sister Morgan helped Nan to clean herself up. Her skirt was dirty from kneeling on the street and her hair was a mess. The Matron agreed that Nan should come in after the weekend and assist one of the more experienced nurses. Before she left the hospital Nan went to the children's ward to check on the little boy. His leg was already in plaster and he was fast asleep. She was curious to know more about him and decided to visit again in the evening.

When Ella told John that his son would not be coming home and that he was throwing up his university course to go on some tom fool expedition to Antarctica he was initially stunned. She did not tell him the real reason why his son would not be coming home, but hinted that he was ashamed of being drunk, hitting that man and getting arrested. At first John thought of contacting the organizers of the expedition and telling them that his son was not suitable to become a member, but then he thought that if the boy was going to start drinking and fighting perhaps it would be better if he was out of the way for a while. He would soon miss his home comforts and learn the hard way how much his parents had done for him.

Perhaps Robert Moreton had been interfering again. It might even be that he suggested this ridiculous expedition idea. After all most of these expeditions require the members to contribute financially, and there was no way that John could have done that without help from Moreton. John was becoming increasingly angry about the squire's interference in his family's affairs. So far as Nan's disappearance was concerned, he put it down to her breeding; she had a renegade father and a wayward mother after all.

Whenever John needed to think things through he inevitably made for the hills and now was no exception. As he walked through the village and up the footpath leading to the Long Hill he considered the recent events. His son's behaviour merely added to his view that the new century was going from bad to worse. At first there had been that ridiculous war against the Boers in South Africa. He had never been convinced about imperialism and when heard about those farmers turned soldiers making a mockery of the British Army, and those dreadful camps used to detain the Boer families, he was disgusted. Of course the Empire eventually triumphed, but at what cost. Many British soldiers had been killed or injured and the morale of the army had been badly dented. Then the old Queen had died and her dissolute son became king. What an example he was, with his mistresses and his pleasure seeking lifestyle. Then there was the growing rivalry between Britain and Germany. Where was that going to lead?

John's head was so full of these thoughts that he walked much too quickly up the steep slope of the hill and found himself gasping for breath at the top. There was also that throbbing in his temples, which seemed to distort his vision momentarily until his breathing returned to normal and he was able to continue walking more slowly along the top of the hill. As he looked down into the valley he thought for a moment about Ella. When she had told him about his son she had seemed to use a tone almost of contempt. Things had never been the same between them since Amy's death. She blamed him for turning the girl away when she was bearing that child and this was compounded when he refused to allow Amy's body to be brought back to the village for burial. She had instead been interred in the new graveyard at Llanwddyn above the artificial lake. It was easier then to maintain the fiction so far as the village was concerned that his stepdaughter had died abroad of some exotic sounding disease and that they had brought her child back with them out of the goodness of their hearts.

Of course Ella would miss her granddaughter very much. They had always been close. In fact he had often felt that the child had come between him and his wife. Perhaps now that she had gone they might have a better relationship again. He wondered briefly where Nan had gone, and how she would manage on her own, but then decided as the saying goes that having made her bed she must lie in it. He had given her every opportunity to make good, with extra help with her schooling, and the chance to become a pupil teacher which she had rejected. The girl had a good brain, he knew that. Well, now she must make her own way in the world.

When Nan left the hospital she walked back beside the church, crossed the road where that car had knocked down the little boy, made her way along a narrow cobbled side-street, into another churchyard, past a well- known hotel, down some steep stone steps, through an ancient passageway, where the upper storeys of the old buildings jutted out over her head, and came out at last into the old Market Square. The market had moved to new premises a short walk away, but the square was still full of people, mainly men, who seemed to be gathered around a woman standing on a chair. Nan moved closer to hear what the woman was saying and caught the words, 'Vote' and 'Rights' between the jeering of the men around her. The woman was tall and slim, well dressed, in a pale coloured skirt, a white blouse stained with what looked like egg yolk and she wore a wide straw hat, with a squashed tomato caught on the brim. Nan knew that this was one of the new militant women suffragettes and she admired her courage.

Ella had often told Nan about her mother's passionate views on women's suffrage, but in those days the movement had been more restrained, merely attempting through meetings with, and letters to Members of Parliament, and other influential people, to gain their support. But now New Zealand and Australia had given women the vote while in England things remained the same. Women had become frustrated and tactics had changed. Under the leadership of Mrs Pankhurst women had taken to the streets, trying to spread their message to the general public, and there had been incidents, such as that where a woman had chained herself to some railings and been arrested by the police. Earlier this year Nan had read in John's newspaper about a protest march, where the weather had been dreadful and the women's clothing had become so soiled so that the event became known as the Mud March.

The woman's voice was becoming shrill as she tried to be heard above the heckling and her rather hard face had become flushed as the men taunted her.

'Come on, Darling. Lift up your skirts. Let's see if you'm a proper woman.'

'D'you go on at your old man like that, when you'm in bed.'

'Nah. She ain't married. Who'd ave er?

Each of these remarks was followed by crude laughter, but the woman went on undeterred. Nan tried to move closer to hear what she was saying. She pushed a little way into the crowd, upset on the woman's behalf and blushing at the men's remarks. Suddenly she felt a hand touching her thigh. She looked round quickly at the men closest to her, but they all assumed innocent expressions and showed their hands as if to say, 'It wasn't me'. Nan squirmed her way out of the crowd and moved quickly away.

As she crossed the square she began to think about her mother. Ella had often told her about Amy, but now she had a longing to know much more. John never spoke about her at all and her Uncle John's memories were from a young boy's point of view. She knew from photographs that her mother had been pretty, with long golden hair, a graceful figure and a lovely smile. Nan knew from Ella's remarks that she herself had inherited her father's darker looks. Of course she knew even less about him, though Ella had told her as much as she could. She did not share her husband's bitter hatred of the man called Huw, but of course Ella had never really known him, having only glimpsed him at the entrance to the tower as the police hurried him away.

Nan felt quite weary as she walked back up Pride Hill. It had been an eventful day, but a productive one too. She would be able to tell Agnes that she had found her voluntary work, though she would not tell her yet that she would soon be moving into the nurse's home as a proper student nurse.

When she reached the top of the hill she decided to return to the hospital. It was not an official visiting time, but perhaps they would let her have a brief word with the boy. She used Sister Morgan's name to gain access to his ward and there he was sitting up, whistling softly. At first she hardly recognised him, because his face had been washed and his hair brushed, but just as she reached the bed he turned and gave her a smile of recognition that left no doubt.

'Hello, there. How's the leg?'

'It 'urts. But not half what it did.'

'What's your name?'

'Alfred. What's yours?'

'Nan'

'You're very pretty, Nan.'

He spoke with such maturity, that Nan blushed, as if he had been a man.

'Have they told your parents about your accident?'

'Aint got none. Well, me mum's dead. And me dad's dead drunk most of the time.'

'So who looks after you?'

'I do.'

Nan frowned.

'Oh it's all right. I got 'a place to stay, wiv me Gran. She's a good sort, but 'er 'ealth aint too good these days.'

'How do you manage for money?'

'I get's odd jobs, collects bottles to return, finds things 'an that.'

Nan brought the two coins out of her skirt pocket.

'I think these might be yours.'

It was Alfred's turn to blush, but he took the coins.

'Ta!'

A nurse was walking towards them, with a stern look on her face.

'Look, I'd better go. It's not really visiting time.'

She turned to the Nurse.

'When do you think Alfred will be going home?'

'Oh that's his name is it? He told us it was Charles. Sooner the better. He's trouble that one.'

Nan asked for a pencil and a scrap of paper from the Nurse, wrote her new name and address on it and handed it to the boy.

As Nan left the ward he heard the boy say to the nurse.

'I can't read. What's it say?'

'It's the lady's name, Mrs Mary Brown, and her address.'

Nan had left the ward when the boy muttered, 'So I aint the only one as tells lies'.

Nan reached the station and began to follow the footpath which would take her back to Castlefields, but then changed her mind and walked into the station instead. She had never visited her mother's grave. John would not go there and Ella could not face what she thought of as a long journey. She knew that her mother was buried at a place in Wales sounding like a sort of soap but she didn't know how to spell it, but she remembered the name of the lake, which was Vyrnwy. She asked at the ticket office how she could get there and the man in the booth explained.

'Your nearest station is Llanfyllin. Change at Gobowen for the Cambrian Railway. When you get to Llanfyllin you must take a cab the rest of the way. When are you going?'

Chapter Eleven

It was after midnight when Philip finally left the Adelphi and went to his own lodgings. We agreed to meet again next day for lunch in a city centre restaurant. He was waiting for me next day and after ordering our meal he said, 'So you reached Chicago and spent the night in Cindy's rooms. What happened next?'

'When I woke I was alone. Jed's bed on the floor had been folded up and taken away. I wondered for a moment whether he had abandoned me in Chicago. But then I heard sounds from Cindy's bedroom that suggested that old acquaintance was being renewed. I smiled and went back to sleep.

Later that day Cindy took Jed to the theatre where she was a valued member of the chorus and introduced him to the manager. On the strength of his experience with Buffalo Bill's Wild West Show he was given a slot in the second half where, dressed in a splendid cowboy costume, he regaled the audience with stories of the old west, a song or two, and an exhibition of marksmanship. I went to see the show on the third night and was astonished by his showmanship. He held the audience entranced with his stories and they were delighted by his songs and encouraged to join in when the words appeared on a screen at the back of the stage. I noticed the catch in his voice and perhaps a tear in his eye as he sang,

"Oh give me a home where the buffalo roam
And the deer and the antelope play..."

When the audience joined in with the chorus they nearly raised the roof, and when Jed's act ended there was loud applause.

When Cindy appeared on stage to dance and sing with the chorus I could see how Jed had been attracted to her in the first place. In her ordinary clothes she was pretty enough but in that spangled costume showing most of her legs she was very attractive indeed. I began to wonder whether Chicago was to be the end of our journey, or at least of Jed's, because I longed to go on to Wyoming.

I also got a job, not as glamorous as Jed's, humping carcases about in a slaughterhouse. It was cold, tiring, dirty work, but soon I had saved enough dollars for the rest of the journey to Wyoming in the comfort of a proper railway carriage. After a few weeks I decided to have things out with Jed. It looked as though he had it made, but I could not go on sleeping on Cindy's sofa and hearing their frequent lovemaking without feeling increasingly embarrassed and frustrated. But in the end it was Jed who made the change. One day he asked me to meet him at the theatre after the show, and took me to a bar nearby. Putting our beers down on the table he said, 'Time to move on.'

'You mean I should find a place of my own.'

'No, I mean we should both travel on to Wyoming.'

'But Cindy...'

'Well, Cindy's been talking marriage and I aint the marrying kind.'

A few days later there was a tearful parting between Cindy and Jed on the platform at Chicago Central but at last he shook her off, and stepped onto the train just as it pulled away. Soon we were crossing the immense prairies at the heart of the continent; mile after mile of rolling grassland, isolated ranches and huge herds of roaming cattle. Jed was very quiet for a while and I wondered if he was regretting his decision, but then he spotted two horsemen in a cloud of dust as they galloped across the plains. His face broke into a smile, 'Gee, how I miss the feel of a horse between my legs.'

I dozed and when I woke the landscape beyond the carriage window looked exactly the same, as if we hadn't moved but when I checked my watch I discovered that we had been travelling for nearly a whole day. At last the train pulled into the station at Omaha City. We got out to stretch our legs and find a bite to eat while the two locomotives which had pulled our train from Chicago took on more coal and water. The sight of those shiny black lumps of coal being shovelled into the tenders made me think about the mines of Wyoming, where I hoped to find work. It seemed to me that I had been on the move almost for ever, certainly since I had landed in New York. There had been hardly time to look back at all. I had rarely given a thought to people back home, had never even written to Philip to say where I was or what I was doing. Suddenly I was filled with guilt, about my dear sister Nan, whose whereabouts I did not know, and I thought of Amy, though I blamed her equally for not trying to contact me.

When the train moved on again night was falling and as we travelled on through the darkness I began to wonder where I was heading, what lay in store for me, and –I suppose it was the unbroken blackness beyond the window- I was filled with apprehension and regret. At last I slipped back into a fitful sleep and dreamt about that tower at the side of the lake, where I was trapped with Amy as the water crept slowly upwards. In my dream I was on my own but when I looked down into the swirling water I saw Amy's body sinking slowly. I leapt into the water to save her, but suddenly woke to find Jed shaking me.

'Wake up, Huw. We're almost there. Cheyenne at last.'

At Cheyenne, the capital city of Wyoming, we left the railroad and travelled by stagecoach through towns with names -Laramie, Elk River, Bitter Creek- that reminded me of Jed's talks about the Wild West. At last we reached the town of Green River and spent the last of our money on a slap up meal and a night in a seedy hotel.

Next day we turned away from the river which flowed through the town and set off to walk to Jed's ranch – about fifty miles he reckoned - across the open uninhabited plains. It was the hottest time of the year so we travelled in the early morning and at sundown, spending the rest of the day lying up in whatever shade we could find. Jed's skills as a rancher become absolutely essential: he used the stars to navigate; he knew where to find water and whether it was suitable to drink; he used his pistol to get us an occasional meal and he made sure there were no lurking dangers, such as rattlesnakes or pumas around when we set up camp.

After a week or so we reached the ranch. Jed's parents were overjoyed. They welcomed him like the prodigal son, with literally the fatted calf, and because I was his friend they made me equally welcome. Both his parents were in their seventies: the father tall and slim like his son, but with his back slightly bent from years of hard work. his legs bowed from so much time spent on horseback and his face rutted like a dried up river bed and brown as mud from all the time spent outdoors; the mother was small and slight and she peered through thick spectacles because her sight was going, but her brain was as sharp as a honed blade.

Jed's older brother Ben was not so welcoming. Since Jed went east with Buffalo Bill he had run the ranch exactly as he wished and that's how he wanted it to stay. He hardly spoke to his brother and looked at me with utter contempt, making fun of my short stature and my strange accent. He was a handsome man, several years older than Jed, but his face held a permanent scowl and an ugly scar disfigured one side of his sunburned face, a souvenir from the Sioux wars of the eighteen seventies, when he joined the army as a very young man. His wife Daisy was trying to be loyal to her husband but you could see that her natural friendliness was struggling under this constraint. She was pretty woman about half her husband's age. I discovered that they had been married for about four years and wondered why no children had yet come along.

Jed tried to make a rancher of me, to no avail. Horses took an instant dislike to me and the herds of long horned cattle eyed me with malicious intent, so Jed got me mending fences, fixing the roof tiles, and helping his mother and Daisy with the chickens. It was obvious that Ben's opinion of me plummeted with every example of my incompetence, but what worried me more was the way his young wife began to follow me around and kept glancing at me over the dining table. I began to think it was time to move on.

A couple of months after our arrival at the ranch the decision was made for me. Ben and Jed had gone to the far side of the ranch to deal with some cattle rustling and would not be back till the next evening. When I made for my bed I found that it was already occupied. It was Daisy, in a pretty nightgown, with her dark gold hair loose around her shoulders. I sat on the bed and whispered, 'Daisy, you must go back to your room at once. This isn't right.'

She sat up in the bed and looked at me, with tears in her eyes.

'You're a good man, Huw. Take me away from here please.'

'Why? What's wrong?'

'Let me show you.'

She turned her back to me and lifted up her flimsy nightdress and I saw the dark, hand shaped bruises on her back. I was shocked but also aroused by the fine curves of her white flesh. I was longing to reach out and touch her but I knew what would happen if I did and knew that if Ben found out he would kill me or Daisy or both.. .

'Ben did that?'

She let the nightgown fall back over her body and turned to face me. She nodded and muttered, 'Many times'

'But why?'

'Because he can't do what he wants to do. He aint a proper man see. His face weren't the only thing them injuns damaged. So when he can't do it he gets angry and takes it out on me.'

'Has he always been like that?'

'Pretty much. Course I didn't know when I married him.'

My desire for this lovely young woman turned to anger against her husband.

'Is there any where you could go where Ben wouldn't find you?'

'I got a friend in Chicago. Ben don't know about her. He don't like me having friends.'

'Would she take you in?'

'Oh sure. We were at school together. We write often, but I get her letters delivered elsewhere. Lucy and me are pretty close.'

'OK, this is the plan. You go back to your room, get dressed and pack a change of clothes. Have you got money for the fare to Chicago?'

'Ben don't give me no money. Says I'm too stupid... But I know where he keeps his cash. Reckon I deserve some of that for what he done to me.'

'When that big clock in the hall sounds midnight, meet me behind the barn. I'll hitch up the buggy and take you to Green River. We'll be long gone before Ben gets back.'

Daisy put her arms round me and kissed me on the mouth. It had been a long time since I had been that close to a woman, especially one as sweet and pretty as Daisy, and I was tempted to lay her back down on the bed and earn my reward, but instead I pulled her off the bed and gave her a gentle push towards the door of my room and whispered urgently.

'Go! Now!'

When we met behind the barn Daisy's face shone in the moonlight and her smile told me that she was feeling like someone just released from jail. I knew that feeling. We boarded the buggy and walked the horse till we were out of earshot, then I cracked the whip and we were away. Daisy hugged me, partly out of gratitude but also because the buggy swayed and bucked violently along the rutted track. Every ten miles or so I halted the buggy to rest the horse and give it chance to feed from the meagre grass, fresh with dew. When this happened Daisy and I would get down and sit on a horse blanket that had been left in the buggy, sharing a bottle of sarsaparilla and a piece of pie she had stolen from the larder. Sitting side by side with her in the moonlight I was tempted to give way to my frustrations, and I felt sure that she would have allowed it, but I knew that if I did I would become responsible for Daisy and I didn't feel ready for that.

We travelled through the night and most of the next day, arriving just in time for Daisy to catch the last coach to Cheyenne. She waved as the coach drew away in a cloud of dust. I hoped sincerely that she would find her friend and be able to make a new life for herself and wondered if my own wanderings would ever cease.

Chapter Twelve

I took the horse and buggy to some stables and asked the owner to contact Jed and tell him where it was. Jed had given me a few dollars pay for my help around the ranch, far more than I deserved, so I had enough to pay for food and drink for a few days, but from now on I would have to travel on foot. I didn't need a map. I knew that if I followed the river upstream I would eventually come to that valley I had been dreaming about for so long.

For two days I followed the river as its course wound towards the wall of mountains in the west from where it flowed. I passed through a couple of small towns where I bought provisions, and at night I slept under the stars beside the river, its tune changing day by day from a soft lapping to a noisy rushing as it narrowed and flowed more swiftly among the rising hills. The air began to cool a little and the valley turned green with trees at the water's edge and lush meadows above. In everything but scale I could be back in my Welsh homeland. My spirits rose.

On the third day I saw the first of the mines. These were simple affairs, where the coal came to the surface on the hillside. I learned later that these were called drift mines. The coal was extracted by the farmers who owned the land, for their own use and for any neighbours who were prepared to get the coal for themselves.

The valley widened out slightly and I came to a slightly larger town built around a bridge, which took a busy road across the river. I was running short of cash, so I bought some bread and cheese and made my way on again, hoping I might soon find a place to work and somewhere to sleep because the nights were becoming cooler. Now the valley sides steepened again. Ahead of me the mountains loomed, some of the highest peaks already topped with snow. The river below me bubbled and spumed over boulders. There were no longer many trees beside it. Instead there were water meadows where a few cattle and horses grazed, and a little higher up would be a farm house surrounded by barns and outhouses and above that scrawny sheep nibbled at the sparser grass on the steep hillsides.

My path had been climbing upwards for most of the day. I stopped to rest for a while and eat my meagre meal, before moving on again. It was some time since I had last seen a farm below me. By late afternoon I was tired and hungry and was beginning to wonder if I would ever see another human habitation, when just ahead of me I saw another of those mines. This one seemed rather more substantial than the rest, with a proper timber framework covering the entrance, like a large porch. Near this entrance stood a wagon half filled with coal and balanced on the coal was a tall man with white hair and a long white beard. The man was singing while he directed a younger man, possibly his son, for he was even taller than the old man and had a cloud of fair curls about his head as he shovelled coal into the wagon. They were so intent on their task that I drew close enough to hear the words of the older man's song and I was stunned when I realised that the tune was one I knew and that the words were in Welsh.

'Noswaith dda,' I called out. Both men turned towards me, the older one with a smile, saying, 'Pwy dach chi?' while the younger one glared and asked, 'Who the hell are you?'

'Huw Morris dew i.'

The old man climbed down slowly from the wagon, came towards me, and offered his hand, asking, 'Sut dach chi, Huw?'

I told him that I was fine, in Welsh. By now the younger man had joined us and seemed to have lost some of his suspicion. The old man introduced himself and his son and explained that they had better continue the conversation in English because Davy did not follow the Welsh so well because he had been only a baby when they had left the valleys of South Wales.

'I am called Geraint and this is my son Daffydd, though he prefers to be called Davy. But what on earth brings you all the way to the Green River Valley, Huw?'

'Oh, that's a long story.'

'Well then,' said Geraint, 'You had better come down to the farm and tell us your story over a meal. My wife and daughter will be delighted. We rarely see anyone up here and a Welshman...'

I was introduced to Ceinwen, Mrs Lloyd and Branwen, their daughter, and as we shared a superb lamb stew I told them my story, missing out my prison sentence. I noticed that Davy listened intently as I told my story and afterwards when we moved onto the verandah for a smoke he asked, 'So you worked in the slate quarries,Huw?'

'Yes. At first I was just a labourer but later I became a skilled fireman.'

'So you can handle explosives?'

'Oh yes.'

'Do you know, Huw. I think you may be the answer to our prayers. See, the farm hardly pays for itself. The soil's too thin up here and it gets mighty cold in the winter, with deep snow for months. I've been wanting to turn the mine into a proper business. Most people don't realise how valuable the coal is. There used to be forests all round here, but most of the timbers been felled. That town you came through, well it's growing rapidly. People are passing through all the time, on their way west to make a new life for themselves. There's new hotels going up everywhere.

He paused to relight his pipe, then went on.

'See, Dad's getting too old for getting the coal and I aint no good with explosives. Shit scared in fact. But if you joined us, reckon we could make something of it. What d'you think?'

'Sounds good to me.'

I stayed with the Lloyds for nearly two years. At first I slept in the barn, then Geraint built a bed for me in the living room and Ceinwen fixed up a curtain to give me some privacy. Davy and I got a good business going. We painted a sign on the wagon, 'Lloyd and Morris, purveyors of best quality coal.' I knew just the right amount of explosive to use. Davy always disappeared when I lit the fuse, but he was powerfully built and could fill a wagon in no time, with me doing my best to help.

I got to know the family very well. Geraint must have been much like his son when he was younger. Even now he had a fine physique, but painful arthritis had slowed him down. Ceinwen reminded me of my mother before she got ill. She was small and slight, with her long silver hair pinned up in a bun, but she was full of nervous energy. Branwen was a couple of years younger than her brother, but very different in looks and manner. Instead of his mass of fair curly hair, hers was long and straight and deep brown. She had a fine figure, a lovely face and a serenity that was very calming to those around her.

The Lloyds had left the valleys of South Wales twenty years before. Geraint's father had died from the coal dust and his brother had been killed in a roof fall down the mine. Geraint was determined that he would not share their fate, so they had braved the Atlantic, with a very young Davy in his mother's arms, and made their way across the continent, aiming for the West coast, but they were forced to stop in Green River while Branwen was born. Geraint was given work at one of the mines- no going underground here- and then found this farm which was derelict at the time. With his tremendous energy and a capacity for hard work he had brought the farm back to life. They had lived here ever since.

Ceinwen, like my mother, loved to tell the old stories, but she had learned them from her mother and grandmother, rather than reading them in books as my mother had done. During the dark winter evenings she would tell these stories, sometimes in English and sometimes in Welsh. She had a wonderful skill at the storytelling. We would all sit round the stove, which burned brightly with coal from the mine, and share her stories. I remember one in particular, about Saint Dwynwen.

'Dwynwen lived long, long ago. She was said to be one of twenty four children fathered by Brychan Brycheiniog who was then King of Wales. She was known everywhere for her purity and her religious zeal.'

'She fell in love with a handsome young man called Maelor and they wanted to marry, but her father refused consent as he wanted to arrange a marriage for her with another, much richer suitor. In his anger about the rejection Maelor raped Dwynwen and left her.'

'Dwynwen went into the nearby woods to seek consolation. She prayed to God to rid her of her feelings for Maelor. In answer to her prayers an angel appeared to Dwynwen in a dream and gave her a potion to help her to forget Maelor and turn him to ice.'

'Then God granted Dywnwen three requests. She was so kind=hearted that her first request was that Maelor should be thawed out, even though he had treated her so badly. Her second request was that God would look kindly on the hopes and dreams of all young lovers. Finally she asked that she would never marry. All these wishes came true so she devoted the rest of her life to God.'

'She became a nun and settled on Llanddwyn Island, off the coast of Yns Mon, or Anglesey as it is now known. When she died a church was built in her honour and it is now a place of pilgrimage for young lovers seeking assurance about their future lives together.'

When Ceinwen finished her tale she sighed and closed her eyes for a moment. Branwen and I glanced at one another and smiled. She had become my friend, then more than a friend. When I slept in the barn she had visited me there, and even when I moved into the house we would find times to be together in the barn. Soon we had an unspoken agreement that we would eventually marry. But alas, it wasn't to be.

Davy might well have been a hero from one of those old stories. He was immensely strong and was never happier than when performing some physical task; shovelling huge piles of coal or digging ditches in the rocky soil. In fact the only time he became morose was when the weather was too bad for him to go out. Then he would pace about the house until his mother persuaded him to sing. He had a fine tenor voice and he would sing louder and louder until the house seemed to shake, but when Branwen joined in he would soften his voice so that they blended together in a wonderful harmony. Oh Branwen! Branwen.

When we went down to the town to deliver the coal I saw a very different Davy. He took a change of clothes with him and when we had finished unloading the wagon he would go the bathhouse, wash off the coal dust, dress in his best clothes and have his hair cut. After that he visited the saloon for several drinks and made his way to Miss Brown's establishment. The first time he did this I accompanied him. When he rang the bell a bevy of young girls, some only half dressed, came to the door and when they saw who it was they screamed with joy Now I knew what sort of a place it was I retired to one of the hotels, had a good meal and a drink or two, then swept out the wagon and slept in it till Davy returned. It was late by the time he reappeared, then he would take my place in the wagon and snore like a dragon while I drove back to the farm.

Davy had been right about the need for coal in the expanding town. We could sell as much as we could get, especially to the hotels, filled with travellers, escaping from the eastern states where the economic depression was still continuing, to try their luck in the west. By the summer of my second year with the Lloyds I had managed to put money in one of the banks and in another year or so I reckoned I could put down a deposit on a small farm for Branwen and me.

One day in August 1897 we took the wagon down to the town as usual, and delivered a load of coal to the River View Hotel. It was hard work in the heat but at last we had finished. Davy went off for his customary entertainment and I went into the hotel and ordered a steak and a couple of beers. By the time I had finished my meal I was ready for a snooze, but when I reached the wagon I saw this guy reading the sign on the side. He had his back to me and his face was in shadow under a wide Stetson hat but there was something familiar about him. I tapped him on the shoulder and when he looked round I saw that it was Jed. He smiled broadly and said, 'Howdy Huw. I knew there couldn't be more than one Morris in this god forsaken place.'

'What are you doing here?' I was pleased to see him, but worried that he had come to find Daisy.

'Is that the way to greet an old friend. Aint you going to buy me a drink. It's been a damned hot journey.'

So I went back with him into the hotel and ordered some beers. When I took them to the table I asked, 'So how's things on the ranch?'

Jed took a good pull at his beer, then answered, 'Not good at all. See, the old man died last winter. Left the ranch to Ben, and he's been a bastard since Daisy disappeared.' Then he gave a wry smile and added, 'Of course you don't know where she is, I suppose?'

' 'Fraid not. I didn't even know she'd gone till you just told me.'

'That's strange. See, she left the very same day as you. And the buggy went missing too. Naturally Ben thought you and her had left together. The names he called you would have blistered your ears. He reckoned you'd gone back east and taken her with you,'

I was really pleased that Daisy had managed to get away and hoped that things were going well for her.

Jed asked about my life and I told him about the Lloyd's. When I mentioned Branwen he smiled. 'She sweet on you?'

'Yep, and it's mutual. We plan to marry soon.'

'Oh that's a pity. I was hoping...'

'So why are you looking for me?'

'Well, it aint much good me showing you now, but I will anyways'

He took a crumpled newspaper from his inside pocket and smoothed out the front page on the table.

A large headline announced, 'Gold! Gold! Gold! Beneath this was a map of somewhere called the Yukon way up on the border between northern Canada and Alaska. I read the article beneath this and learned that big finds of gold had been made in that region and thousands of gold seekers were making their way up there.

'You see,' said Jed, 'Dad left the ranch to Ben, but he left me a small inheritance. I'm gonna use it to get me up there and get me some gold. Then I can git a ranch of my own and damn Ben!'

'So what has this got to do with me?'

'Well, I thought you might want to join me. We're good friends and we've shared a lot. It'll be a load of fun. And there's the chance of getting real rich. But I can see that you're doing OK. So I guess I'll have to do it on my own.'

Next I asked the question that I was to regret for some time.

'So how much d'you reckon you'll need to get there and keep going till you find gold.'

'Bout five hundred dollars I guess. Course it's cheaper for two, cause you can share a tent and stuff.'

That was almost exactly the amount I had in the bank. I began thinking. What if I did go with him? I'd only be away a year or so. And if I found gold I could come back and buy a fine farm. Surely Branwen would wait that long?

'When you leaving?

'Soon's I can.'

'Look, I'm going to discuss this with Branwen. If I decide to join you I'll be here outside the hotel at ten tomorrow. If I'm not here you'll know I aint coming. OK?'

In the end I didn't even tell Branwen. I slept in the barn that night, saying it was too hot in the house. Next morning I was up early and on my way down the valley before the sun was up. No wagon this time and it was a good walk. Got my money from the bank, joined Jed on the hotel steps and by noon we were on our way northwards. What a heel!

Chapter Thirteen

It took Jed and me a week to reach Seattle. We walked a good deal of the way to keep our savings. Other times we hitched rides with farmers going in the right direction or simply jumped on the back of loaded wagons without the driver's permission till he stopped to unload. The strange thing is I didn't miss the Lloyds or the farm for a while, or even Branwen. I felt free again. Jed was good company and a sense of adventure seemed to have got into my bones.

As we got close to Seattle the roads became busy with so many people going in the same direction. There were young and old, some families with several children, some who looked like they'd just left their jobs in offices, others from farms with straw in their hair, some rode in carts or buggies, others had handcarts, some had piles of luggage, others just small packs on their backs. But all had one thing in common, the smell of gold in their nostrils.

From a hill just outside the city we could see the bay, filled with all kinds of craft, from paddle steamers to skiffs, taking the opportunity of making money by ferrying the gold seekers northwards towards Skagway and Dyea. We soon heard horror stories about many of the boats being unsuitable, unseaworthy, overcrowded, and sinking on the way. Nevertheless the cost of a ticket rose daily.

Normally Seattle was a bustling port which exported timber from the surrounding hills. Now it was bulging at the seams. But when we got into the city we found that many of the buildings were empty, whole businesses had ceased when the workers had just up and left for the Yukon. Streetcars had been abandoned mid journey while the drivers joined the gold rush. We learned that even the mayor of the city had joined in. We bought what supplies we could, at inflated prices, slept in a newly made park, while we sought a vessel we felt was safe enough to make the journey up that dangerous coast.

At last we made our decision and as our steamer made its way northwards, hugging the mountainous coast, the air began to cool and thick fog formed and dispersed. I had purchased a book in Seattle called 'A Manual for Gold Seekers' which we studied as the boat crawled towards Dyea. From this we learned that when we landed we must make our way along the Chilkoot Trail, and then climb the Chilkoot Pass. We had to take enough supplies with us to last a year, otherwise the Mounties would turn us back at the Canadian border. There were tales of starvation in previous years.

At last we disembarked at Dyea, got our supplies together at ever increasing prices and purchased an old pony to help us carry our load. The weather had changed to continuous rain and as we made our way along the trail the pony's hooves kept slipping in the mud and we found ourselves lightening its load and transferring more and more to our own backs.

There were so many people on the trail that it was like a great army moving towards some distant battle. At times we got in each other's way, but generally our fellow gold seekers were a cheerful, honest lot and there was plenty of banter and song, especially in the camps along the way, because it was impossible to go on when darkness descended.

By now the short Alaskan summer had ended and as we approached the foot of the pass the temperature suddenly dropped and the rain turned to snow. We set up camp for a few days before beginning our ascent. The pony would never make it up the pass so we sold it, for a fraction of what we had paid, to some disillusioned gold seekers who were returning to Dyea. Better than it joining the other carcases in a nearby gulch. Now we had to break up our supplies into smaller bundles and hire some native Klingit tribesmen to carry them upwards. This meant another considerable depletion of our savings, but it would have taken us thirty trips or so to carry the stuff up the pass by ourselves. By the time we were organised the snow had frozen underfoot, which in fact made the track easier to climb. The higher we climbed the heavier the snow fell. This was avalanche territory and later we heard that there had been one a short while after we reached the top and sixty prospectors had been killed.

At a place called the Scales our supplies were weighed and we were allowed to continue into Canadian territory. We hired a boat – more savings gone – and sailed across Lake Lindemann, then reached Lake Bennett at the head of the Yukon, but by the time we reached the shore of that lake the water had begun to freeze. We would not be going any further until winter was over and the ice had melted.

We set up our tent among hundreds of others. The temperature dropped to thirty below zero- we were told it could go as low as fifty- and Jed and I spent the nights lying close together like lovers, except that we remained fully dressed. We spent most days foraging for firewood so that we could make at least one hot meal a day. We made friends with the Braddock family in the next tent, sharing a camp fire and supper, which we each cooked in turn.

Ken Braddock was a large, jovial man, who had driven a locomotive for one of the railroad companies back east, but the company had gone bust, so they had made their way across Canada to seek their fortunes. He still wore his engine driver overalls under his winter clothing and when he sat by the fire in the evening you could still smell the grease and soot from the footplate.

His wife Katy was not the world's best looking woman, with a thin face and ratty hair, but she was the cheeriest, kindest woman you could ever meet and the most loving parent to her son and daughter.

Laura, their twelve year daughter, was big boned and bonny like her father, but Matt, at ten was as skinny as his mother and very pale. Jed and I wondered how they would survive the terrible winter, but the whole family seemed to thrive in the bitter air. In fact it was Jed suffered most. He seemed almost to shrink as the cold got to him and his skin became covered in sores. I think he began to wonder what on earth had driven him to come to this inhospitable place, and frequently apologised for dragging me with him.

In late March, the temperature began to rise slightly and in April the ice began to melt. We decided to share a raft with the Braddocks for the rest of the way down to Dawson City. Much of the timber had been stripped from the surrounding hills, but at last we found enough to make a crude vessel. A party of Mounties came to check on our craft – no one was allowed to sail until each boat or raft had been checked and given a licence – more expense – but at last we were able to load up ready for the journey. The Mounties had warned us that there were some serious rapids at the head of the river and that we should put Mrs B and the children on the shore to walk along the river bank while we negotiated the wild water. We were soon to learn what good advice that was.

At last we were on our way. The raft low in the water as it carried two lots of goldseekers and all their gear. Jed and Ken got the raft going with homemade paddles while I steered with another. The lake was calm and when we reached the head of the river the current helped to increase our speed, but there was still five hundred miles to go.

We made good progress for most of that first day but then the valley narrowed and I heard a sound up ahead, like a gale passing through a wood, and the water began race forward. We pulled the raft over to the river bank, into a backwater behind a large boulder, and Mrs B and the children stepped off the raft and joined a line of people walking along a well-worn path beside the river. Then we manoeuvred the raft back into the current and began to float through the rapids. Suddenly the raft shot forward, completely beyond our control, bucking and swerving like a piece of match-wood, even with the weight of us and our supplies. Luckily we had taken good care to secure everything thoroughly, so now our only concern was to keep ourselves on the raft. Ken's face turned white but his hands were raw red where he grasped a rope. I too lay flat and held on grimly. Jed sat up as if he was riding a bronco and whooped loudly as we sped along. At one point we hit a boulder and I thought the raft would come apart, but at last the valley widened and the water slowed and we were able to steer the raft to a sandy beach and disembark. We were soaked through and shivering from the icy water, so we stripped to our underclothes, stretched our wet clothes out on some boulders and lay on the sand in the warm spring sun. We were still lying there when Mrs B and the children arrived, much to the amusement of Matt and the consternation of a red faced Laura.

This pattern was repeated several times during the next few days. We tightened the ropes about the logs of the raft and fixed our supplies even more firmly. We wore whatever we could find that was vaguely waterproof over our clothes and made handholds for ourselves by threading thin ropes through the logs and so we made good speed down the river. But as we shot through the last rapid disaster struck.

Jed had been getting more and more confident and had begun to try to steer us through the rapids with a paddle held over the back of the raft. We were almost through this one when the raft caught on a rock just below the surface, swung violently round and threw him into the freezing water. He went right under, bobbed up for a moment, then went under again. When his head surfaced again he cried out 'Help..! Can't..!' Then he disappeared again. Dad had taught me to swim in our local lake and I was about to jump in to help Jed when suddenly he stood up in the water, which only came up to his waist and I realised we were through the rapids and into shallower water. Jed struggled out of the river and collapsed on the bank.

Ken and I paddled the raft to the side of the river and joined Jed, who lay on the sand shivering violently. Just then the others arrived. Mrs B. saw Jed lying soaked and shivering, went into hysterics and grabbed her husband. 'It might have been you'. It was Laura who remained cool, stepped onto the raft, brought back blankets to wrap around Jed and said, 'Better get the tents up, Dad. We won't be going anywhere for a while.'

I found a bottle of brandy and forced some down Jed's throat. His colour had changed from white to blue and his whole body was juddering. I remembered that this water had been covered in thick ice just a while ago and became concerned about Jed. The harsh winter had left him weak anyway and I wondered how long it would take him to recover from his total immersion in that icy water.

But the sun grew in strength and after a few days Jed felt sufficiently recovered to continue our journey. He had not slept well since his near drowning and kept moaning through the night about what a fool he'd been to become a gold seeker. He seemed to have lost some of his strength and much of that optimism which had helped us both to survive through thick and thin.

We checked the raft and our supplies. Amazingly we had only lost one pan and a tin of beans. We had been told that there were no more rapids so we all got aboard the raft and let the current carry us down to Dawson.

What a place that was. A short while ago there had been nothing here at all. Now there was a city with between thirty to forty thousand inhabitants. There were some proper buildings, mostly banks, saloons, dancehalls or brothels, but mostly it was just row after row of tents or simple wooden shelters. It was the rowdiest, bawdiest place I'd ever seen, but the Mounties managed to keep control, so law and order prevailed, just.

Jed and I broke up the raft and sold it for firewood. With the money we bought a leaky canoe. The Braddocks had decided to stay in Dawson. Ken had got a job as a doorman at one of the dance-halls. The size of him seemed to deter troublemakers. Mrs B was making and selling her homemade soups – we knew how delicious these were – and Laura's cheerful face encouraged customers. Mathew earned pocket money delivering news sheets. So we bade that family a tearful farewell, loaded our canoe – we had managed to stop the leak at least for now – and went on our way to the Klondike.

What a changed place this was now that spring had arrived. Each day the sun rose earlier and set later. It was dawn by three in the morning and twilight lingered past nine at night. All day long the sun blazed and we sweated in our thick clothing. The ghostly winter silence had given way to the great spring murmur of awakening life.

It came from the things that lived and moved again after the long months of frost. The sap was rising in the pines. The willows and aspens were bursting out in new buds. Shrubs and vines were green again. Crickets sang in the nights and in the days all manner of creeping, crawling things rustled in the warm sun. Partridges and woodpeckers boomed and knocked in the forests. Squirrels chattered, birds sang and the returning wild fowl honked overhead. I felt full of hope and energy again, but it was not the same for Jed. He remained very pale, he lacked any strength and his usual good humour had deserted him.

Partly his mood was caused by the fact that every inch of every creek had already been taken by earlier gold-seekers. We paddled on and on seeking a piece of land that had not already been claimed. At night we erected our tent with the permission of the miners who had claimed that piece of land and on the understanding that we would move on again next day. Through the night Jed moaned in his sleep and the following day did not seem rested at all.

As we paddled on again, mostly just drifting with the current even I began to wonder whether we should turn back before Jed's strength gave out completely. I didn't know what was wrong with him and I continued to hope that the warmth and the plentiful meat from the beasts and fish we had managed to catch and cook would restore his health.

At last we found a small creek, unclaimed as yet, and set up camp. I wondered whether we had moved so far that we were out of the gold bearing region, but next day Jed woke early after having had his least broken sleep for weeks and started digging near the water even before he had breakfasted. Suddenly he whispered, 'Huw. Over here! Quick!'

When I joined him I could see that he was sweating heavily and he had whispered because his voice had almost gone. But he had a broad smile on his face and as my eyes looked down as he directed I saw that glint among the mud at the water's edge and shouted aloud, 'Gold!'

I fetched the pan and we carefully shovelled some mud onto it, then dipped the pan into the flowing stream. Soon the mud washed away and there among the grit were several small nuggets, and once much larger one, of gold. Talk about beginner's luck. We marked the spot, then returned to our tent and breakfasted. Jed was still shivering, but I assumed that it was with excitement this time. It was agreed that I should go back to Dawson and stake our claim. I put the gold into a small leather bag and sewed it into my underclothes. We marked the map, put enough food for a couple of days in the canoe, and I set off. Jed did not show any signs of worry that I might sell the gold and disappear. He knew that I would return as soon as I could.

It took me three days to reach Dawson, against the current. By the time I had staked our claim, banked our gold and set off back to our camp almost a week had passed. When I reached the creek there was no sign of Jed. I had expected to see him by the water's edge, washing away the mud and gathering more gold. I beached the canoe and called for him but there was no answer. I reached the tent and looked inside. He seemed to be sleeping. Good, I thought, he needed that. I was tired myself and crawled into the tent beside him. Then I became aware of his utter stillness. One of his hands lay on the blankets that covered him. I touched it and felt how cold it was. I bent over to listen for his breathing, but knew I wouldn't hear any. It was obvious that Jed was no longer alive.

For a while I was devastated. Jed had always been the leader; he always knew what to do. His courage, his sense of adventure had brought us to this place. He had achieved what he set out to do, but now he could not share the spoils.

With the help of a neighbouring gold seeker I buried Jed among the trees that reached almost down to the water's edge. I buried his few possessions with him. The only thing I kept was his gun and some ammunition. I returned to Dawson and informed the authorities of Jed's demise. I sold my claim and the gold we had found for fifty thousand dollars. It was probably worth more but I didn't care. I wanted to leave the place as soon as I could.

I looked up the Braddocks and was amazed to find that instead of a tent they now had a simple hut that doubled as a dwelling and a small diner, which was full of customers. Laura was an efficient waitress. Ken had joined his wife in the kitchen, but Matthew was attending a recently established school. They were saddened to hear about Jed. I did not tell them about the gold, but I pressed a few hundred dollars into Ken's hand and left before he could refuse.

That night I wrote to Branwen, giving the address of the cheap hotel where I was staying, explaining about my good fortune and asking her to marry me. Ten days later her answer came.

'Huw,

I got your letter when I returned from my honeymoon. I was very puzzled and angry when you simply disappeared. Davy advertised for an assistant in the mine and Robert arrived. He is a good man. Dada is not able to work anymore so Davy and Robert work on the farm and the mine together. I help when I can. Robert asked me to marry him. We have built an extension to the farm house. We went to Green River for our honeymoon. I am very happy. Please do not write to me again. I wish you well.

Branwen McDowell (Mrs) '

I did not blame Branwen. How could I? I hoped that Robert McDowell was indeed a good man and that she would continue to be happy. But what about me? What should I do? I had a small fortune but I knew how quickly a fortune could be squandered. I had to make that money work for me, but I didn't know how. If Branwen had married me we could have bought a good sized farm and lived happily ever after - perhaps. But through my own foolishness Branwen was now married to another man.

Then the thought came to me, I could go home, back to Wales. I could find my dear sister, perhaps I could even find Amy and if she had not married I would ask her to marry me. But it had been so long- more than eight years- surely she would have married someone else. I wondered whether we would even recognise one another. But at least I could try to find out what had happened to her. I could easily afford to travel in comfort back to New York and find a ship bound for Liverpool. Next day I started the return journey to Seattle and from there I would travel by rail all the way back to New York.

In Seattle I took out some cash, had a bath and haircut, bought some new smarter clothes – nothing too expensive - a change of clothing, and a suitcase to keep them in. With new clothes on my back and a cheque for a large amount of money in my pocket I suddenly felt vulnerable and was glad of Jed's gun in a holster inside my jacket. I had never fired a pistol and was not sure how accurate I would be, but that weight against my chest was reassuring. Next I bought a ticket to New York. I smiled when I thought of our outward journey, and of Jed sitting opposite me on top of that cattle wagon. Tears filled my eyes as I remembered Jed's self-confidence and his broad smile.

Chapter Fourteen

When I reached New York, which seemed bigger and busier than ever-with buildings reaching higher and higher towards the sky- I went to a bank and opened an account. Now I needed to find somewhere to stay, while I found out about ships bound for Liverpool. I no longer made for the poorer districts, but sought a small hotel in a pleasant neighbourhood, where I took a room with a view over a park. Next day I woke refreshed after the long journey, bathed and breakfasted, then decided to take a stroll before lunch. I made my way along quiet streets, where the summer sun was dappling the sidewalks as it shone through the trees.

I was strolling along when a hansom cab drew up a little ahead of me and a smartly dressed man, of late middle age I guessed, stepped out, paid the driver and walked towards me. The man had a pleasant face, with a healthy tan, smiling blue eyes, surrounded by laughter lines, neatly groomed silvery hair and sideburns. He wore a silk top hat and carried a silver topped cane. His confident stride told me that he was fit for his age. I was surprised when the man greeted me with a smile and 'A fine morning, my friend' He was the kind of man who probably would not have even acknowledged me in my previous garb. After passing me he strode ahead, swinging his cane in one hand and an attaché case in the other.

Suddenly two men came out of an alley and tried to grab the case out of his hand, but it was attached by a chain to his wrist, so that when they pulled at the bag the man lost his footing and fell heavily. I stood dazed for a moment, then remembered the pistol in my pocket. I drew it and advanced quickly towards the two men, shouting, 'Leave him or I'll shoot'

Actually the gun wasn't even loaded, but the men ran away, leaving their victim sprawled on the ground. I put the gun back in its holster and hurried over to him. He sat up, winced with pain and I saw that he had a gash on his forehead, which was bleeding heavily. I took out my handkerchief, folded it and pressed it to the wound.

'Thank you so much, young man. They caught me unawares'

His voice was softer than I would have imagined from such a powerful looking man, probably the result of shock. He winced again.

'I think my wrist is broken. When they snatched my case. Would you take the key from my inside pocket and unlock the chain.'

I found the key and removed the bag from his wrist, which hung limply.

'We'd better get you to a hospital. I'll call a cab.'

'Call a cab by all means. But let it take me home. Doctor Branson can deal with me there.'

Just then I saw a cab enter the street and called it over. The driver was reluctant to stop at first.

'Not another damn drunk.'

Then he recognised the man.

'Why it's Mr Arnstein. Christ Almighty!'

He got down from the cab and together we helped the injured gentleman into the cab. Then almost dismissing me the cabbie said, 'It's OK. I know where Mr Arnstein lives. Everybody does.' But the old man spoke, his voice a little stronger now, 'No, please come back with me. You may have saved my life. The least I can do is offer you a drink.'

I joined him in the cab, more to ensure that he was all right than anything else, and made him as comfortable as I could. The gash on his forehead had stopped bleeding but his face was pale now, almost waxen.

'I'm a damned fool,' he said. 'I've been warned often enough. But I thought it would never happen to me.'

We had only ridden for a couple of streets when the cab drew up outside a splendid house surrounded by trees. Again the driver helped me get Mr Arnstein out of the cab and almost carry him to a large doorway with pillars on either side, where I pulled the bell and heard it ringing somewhere inside. I took a few dollars from my pocket and paid the driver, who walked away just as the door opened and a young woman stood there, for a moment transfixed with shock.

'Father! What on earth!' She quickly regained her calm and called into the house, 'Martha. Come at once!' I was still holding the gentleman by his shoulder so she took his other arm and together we helped him into the house. By now Martha, a heavily built black woman with a white cap sitting ridiculously on top of her tight grey curls, had joined us and when she saw the state of her employer almost went into hysterics. But the young woman spoke calmly, saying, 'Telephone Doctor Branson at once!' and the woman, a servant I presumed, scuttled away. We lowered Mr Arnstein gently onto a comfortable looking sofa in the centre of the hallway, where he sat still and silent, but his face twitching with the excruciating pain. Martha returned saying,

'Doc coming soon. Ten minutes he say.'

While the two women bustled about, Martha fetching a towel and hot water in a bowl, the daughter finding a scarf and making a sling for the broken wrist, I had the opportunity to examine my surroundings, which were more magnificent than any I had ever seen. The hallway was huge. It would have swallowed up the whole of my home in Wales. The floor was marble and a grand staircase rose from it, paused at a landing under a large stained glass window, before splitting and leading off to both sides of the upper floor. I was gazing round in wonder when I heard the old man's voice.

'I don't even know your name, my friend.'

I told him it was Huw.

'And from that accent I guess you're no New Yorker,'

I explained where I came from and that I had been in America for several years.

He placed his good hand on the arm of the young woman who now sat beside him.

'This is my daughter, Julia'

I walked over and shook her hand, studying her properly for the first time. She was older than I had thought, probably about thirty, and no great beauty, but she had good features, large brown eyes and masses of chestnut hair gathered up and held in place with pins. But her most striking feature was her posture which gave her a nobility I had not met before in a woman. She did not speak but gave me a grateful smile, which softened her rather severe face and improved her looks no end.

'These guys just appeared from nowhere and tried to snatch my case. Hey, what happened to my case?'

I had made sure to bring it with me when the cab driver and I helped him to the house. Now I handed it over.

'Thanks again, Huw. You're a regular Good Samaritan, my boy.'

I no longer thought of myself as a boy but I suppose compared with this quite elderly man that is how he saw me.

The doctor arrived, examined the wrist, decided that it was not actually broken, but very badly sprained and bound it up in a most professional manner. He checked the wound on the forehead and decided that it did not need stitches.

'You've done just what was required my dear.'

Julia seemed almost embarrassed by his compliment and turned to speak directly to me for the first time.

'I am most grateful to you. My father is far too trusting. Would you care to join us for lunch, or have you other business to attend to?'

I was happy to accept. All the excitement had given me an appetite.

Branson left to attend to another patient.

Over lunch, a splendid affair, served by Martha in a sumptuous dining room, I was forced to tell the story of my time in America and explain that I was about to recross the Atlantic on my way home.

'That's quite a story, Huw. But at least you found your fortune in our great land,' said Mr Arnstein.

'Not such a fortune really and I know that it I don't use it wisely it will soon disappear.'

'Well, Huw, it's pity you are leaving New York. You see I am an investor- that case of mine was filled with share certificates - and I might well have been able to advise you. Pity. Pity. And also I had thought of offering you a job.'

Julia spoke up, quite fiercely, 'Father, Huw has money of his own. He doesn't want a job.'

I was beginning to like this feisty young woman. Nevertheless, I was intrigued, 'What kind of a job?'

'Well, you see, I learned a lesson this morning. I realise that I am no longer young man and that New York is an increasingly dangerous place. You are young, you look fit and you are probably strong, after all that work in the quarries and the mines. Oh, and it seems you're quite handy with a gun.'

I smiled at this, but didn't deny this. He went on.

'I had hoped that you might become my bodyguard. Just travel with me when I need to go to the office or the exchange. Just keep an eye on me, you know. I'd pay well, and help you to invest that money. My first name's Rudolph, by the way, but most people call me Rudy.'

I could see that Julia was both pleased at the thought that her father had come to his senses about security but offended on my behalf by his offering me employment.

'I am sure that if Huw has made up his mind to return to his homeland, we could find someone else to look after you.'

'But it's about trust, Julia. You see I already know that I can trust this young man.'

I thought for a moment, not so much about the job I had been offered, but about the fact that it would enable me to continue to see Julia, but I needed more information before I made a decision.

'I hope you don't mind me asking, but is there a Mrs Arnstein?'

It was Julia who replied, 'My mother died several years ago, while I was in Europe. I came back to look after Pa. I'm still doing that.'

'And doing it very well,' said her father, touching her hand on the table.

No husband, no fiancé apparently. 'How long will you give me to decide?' I asked.

'Oh, let's say you sleep on it and come and see me in the morning.'

Actually I had already decided, but I shook hands and left.

I hardly knew what an investor did, but when I accompanied Rudy to his office or the stock exchange I listened and learned a little. As he had promised Rudy invested some of my money and showed me how it made more money. 'Not always,' he said. 'You have to know what you're doing. And even then there are times when it all goes wrong. We had a hard time back in '93, but things seem to be on the up again now.'

He gave me a good wage, far more than I deserved for simply following him around. He treated me as a friend rather than as an employee. He told me about his life. His father had come to New York during one of the pogroms in Russia, when the Russian authorities turned against the Jews.

'Terrible times. Terrible times.' muttered Rudy. 'I was just a child. My father arrived with nothing but the clothes on his back, his young wife and me. At first we slept in one room with two other families, but my father was a clever man and a hard worker, by God, and bit by bit he worked his way up in the textile industry, till he got a factory of his own. Momma was not strong and the escape from Russia had broken her health and her nerve. There were no brothers or sisters, so Dad focussed all his energies on me. A good education. A start in the bank of a friend of his. I knew that I had to be successful, for his sake.'

Rudy sighed and was silent for a while.

'Then I met my beloved Dora and soon Julia arrived. But Dora suffered badly when Julia was born, so the pattern was repeated. There were no more children. Julia has been the centre of our lives, our hope for the future.'

With Julia it certainly wasn't love at first sight. I admired her certainly, and she took an interest in me. She took me to concerts at Carnegie Hall, introduced me to Shakespeare. I couldn't make head or tail of him at first, and much preferred the musicals on Broadway. She asked me to accompany her to social events –I assumed this was part of my job- advised me what to wear, introduced me to her friends, helped me to be less self-conscious in smart company. I didn't really enjoy those occasions, I didn't really like most of the people we met. I felt that the only reason they bothered with me at all was because I was with Julia. Most of all I resented those men who were quite obviously making up to Julia simply because she was a very good catch.

One night a particularly odious creep, tall and dark, with his hair smoothed down with oil and a voice that was even more oily, spent the evening making oily eyes at Julia. In the cab on the way back to her house I just couldn't avoid saying, 'I hope you realise that Pilkington chap is only after your money. I gather you're not the first he's tried.'

Julia turned to me, with her eyes flashing in the streetlights.

'You wouldn't be jealous would you, Huw?'

I was stunned into silence. The idea had never occurred to me. Perhaps there was some truth in it.

'I...' I began, but could not go on, because my mind was in turmoil.

It was Julia who spoke next.

'I would like it very much if you were jealous.'

'I don't understand.'

'Oh, Huw, are you really that blind? I've been in love with you since that day you brought my father home.'

The next few years were to be the happiest of my life so far. I soon returned Julia's love for me, in ample measure. The following year we were married, with her father's blessing. We lived with Rudolph, who had begun to show his age, but there was plenty of room for us all. Julia hired a young girl to help out Martha. I discovered that Martha was more of a friend than a servant. She had looked after Julia when she was a baby, because her own mother was weakened by giving birth to her, and they were very fond of one another.

Rudy treated me more as a junior investor now, rather than his bodyguard, and as time went by, I took over more and more of the business from him. I made a few mistakes at first but eventually made a steady income. Meanwhile Julia busied herself with several charities and organised social events. Now that we were married the hangers on had dropped off and I began to meet Julia's real friends. They were a good bunch who worked hard and played hard. We purchased a property out on Long Island and spent our weekends there, sailing, playing tennis or simply entertaining. I seemed to get the hang of being well off pretty quickly and felt only the occasional slight twinge of guilt about the lives of the less fortunate. It didn't seem possible that I had once quarried slate back in Wales in all weathers for a miserable pittance or that I had spent time in one of Her Majesty's jails.

The only thing that remotely marred our marriage was the lack of children, which was surprising considering the time that Julia and I spent being intimate with one another. Then Rudy died, of a sudden, severe heart attack, so that his life ended without too much suffering. Of course Julia was heart-broken and for a while grieved intensively, cutting herself off from everyone, including me to a certain extent. Her father had left the home to Julia and the business to me, so I became a very busy man. Then suddenly, just as we had more or less accepted that we would never have children, Julia became pregnant. It was just what she needed to restore meaning to her life, and for the first few months of her pregnancy she got back to her old self, and bloomed with health. But towards the end of her term things began to go wrong. She developed toxaemia. Rest was recommended and she did as she was told. I began to wonder if there was some physical weakness which had been passed on from her grandmother and her mother, as both had only borne one child, but if the same happened to Julia I did not care so long as she and the baby were fine. But it wasn't to be. The first sign that all was not as it should be, was when Julia's hands, feet and face began to swell. Then she began to suffer from headaches and gastric pain. I hardly liked to leave her to go to the office, even though she was attended regularly by the doctor and Martha was always at hand.

One day I had to travel to Washington to discuss some important business with a couple of bankers, when a message came that I must go home at once. It was the middle of winter and my train got stuck in a snowdrift for a whole night. When I finally got home it was too late. Julia had suffered convulsions and gone in to a coma. Both she and the baby were dead.

At first I just wanted join them in the tomb. Spring didn't happen for me that year. By the time summer came I had sold the business and the house, arranged a good pension for Martha and moved into a small apartment, overlooking the harbour, until could decide what to do. I began to wonder if I was jinxed; first it was Jed, then Julia. Was I destined always to lose those people I was close to, and never have a child of my own?

I spent most of the following year looking out of the window of my apartment, watching the ships arriving and departing, the tugs guiding them across the harbour and the gulls wheeling about their sterns. There was nothing to keep me in New York anymore. Should I try a new life in a new land? Then one night I had an exceptionally vivid dream. I was back at Ty Craig looking out from the porch to a fence, where two young women leaned across the top rail, looking at the animals. One had long fair hair, which curled down her back like the source of a mountain stream; the other's hair was equally long but very dark and straight. Suddenly the women turned to one another and laughed at something one of them had said, then they both turned right round to face me and called out, 'Huw.' When I woke up I dressed and went down to the shipping office and booked my ticket on the Lady of Shallot and here I am.'

Philip, who had listened to the whole of my tale without interrupting, now spoke for the first time.

'That is an incredible story, Huw.'

He took a large gulp from the brandy glass he had been twirling in his fist, as he had listened, engrossed in my story, then spoke again.

'Now I have to add to your sorrows I'm afraid, Huw. You see, Amy too is dead, has been for many years.'

My eyes filled with tears. I remembered Amy as she had been in my dream; so young and lovely. How could she possibly be dead?

Philip finished off his brandy and put down the glass.

'But,' he said, 'I have some good news as well. You see your wish for a child has been granted. You and Amy had a child. She was four years old when Amy died. Amy named her Nan after your sister. Ella insisted that the child came to live with them at Hope Underhill, despite John's protests. Ella has written to me from time to time about the girl. John would not allow the girl to take his name, so she goes by her mother's name. Now your daughter, Nan Morris, is seventeen.'

Chapter Fifteen

When I woke next morning, it was much later than usual for me, because I had been unable to get to sleep, thinking about Amy's death and the child we had made. Philip had suggested that the one person who might be able to tell me more about Amy and my daughter, Nan, would be George Owen.

George had been fifteen when I last saw him. He and his grandmother, Megan, lived in the old village of Llanwddyn. My father and I had the job of demolishing that village before the valley was flooded. Most of its inhabitants had left by the time we arrived with our tools and explosives and set up camp nearby. We soon became friendly with Mrs Owen and young George so we left their house standing until last. But she knew that she would have to move eventually and she had asked her old friends John Noble and his wife to come from England and help her with the move. But in fact it was John and his stepdaughter Amy who arrived.

It was soon obvious that young George had a schoolboy crush on Amy and I must admit I used his infatuation for my own ends, asking him to deliver a letter to her, when her stepfather refused to allow her to see me anymore. The problem had been caused by Philip, who had also fallen for Amy, and had reported something he had seen when the three of us had climbed the mountain of Cadair Idris together. Philip had been jealous because Amy had chosen me and he had seen us in an embrace on top of the mountain, having sneakily followed us when he was supposed to have been resting near the lake below.

Amy was angry with her stepfather for forbidding any further contact with me. She had packed a small suitcase and when it was dark she had come to meet me near the straining tower. She suggested that we run away together, but we were both ambushed by some Welsh nationalists whom I had refused to help with their plan to blow up the tunnel which was being cut through the mountain to carry the water to Liverpool. They thought we would betray them so they locked us in the tower, intending to release us when they had blown up the tunnel But they were all killed because they did not know how to safely use the explosive they had stolen from me. So Amy and I were forced to stay in the tower for that night and the next day and into the next night as the waters of the lake rose towards the temporary floor the builders had constructed to enable them to finish the tower. Amy thought she was going to die and asked me to make a woman of her before this happened. We made love twice before we were released from the tower and I was taken away by the constabulary and never saw Amy again.

Now I had learned that our intimacy had led to the birth of a daughter, who had been named Nan by Amy, after my sister, whom she had met and liked when she and John came to stay in our little farm near the lake of Tal-y-llyn. I had known nothing of the terrible troubles that Amy had suffered because of her pregnancy, after her stepfather had sent her away from her home. Philip had told me briefly about her death five years later by the side of the lake which had formed in the Vyrnwy valley, but he did not know the details, so it was George who could tell me about that tragedy and anything else he knew about my daughter.

George had been a clever boy with a particular interest in engineering. A legacy had enabled him to go to a good school and when that legacy ran out Philip's father, Joseph, took George under his wing, perhaps as a replacement for Philip who had become estranged from his father. So George had gone to live with Joseph in Liverpool in term time and study at the mechanic's institute. Then he had been taken on as an apprentice by a shipping company and according to Philip was now one of their most respected engineers.

So after breakfast I met up with Philip and we made our way to the offices of the White Star line in St James's Street. The building was still quite new and very fine, with alternating bands of pink and cream brick and a sort of tower on each corner. In the vestibule a huge mosaic of a map of the world was set into the floor and a magnificent staircase wound up to the many floors above.

I went up to the reception desk and asked to see George Owen. As the man behind the desk took our names he looked me up and down and decided that I was respectable – probably a shipping magnate or some such – and that Philip was familiar to him on some way, so he asked us to wait on the comfortable seats in the waiting area while he established the whereabouts of Mr Owen. He made a call on the internal phone and came over to us shaking his head.

'I'm afraid Mr Owen is not here at the moment. He is at the shipyards in Belfast, but he is due back later today.'

In my impatience to discover more about my daughter I could not help but mutter, 'Damn it!' then when I looked at the man's stricken face I smiled, put on a more obvious American accent and said, 'Sorry about that. We Americans have no manners.'

The man seemed placated and strode back to his desk. I turned back to Philip and asked, 'So what do we do now?'

'We find out when his boat arrives and wait at the docks.'

I was so grateful that Philip seemed to have abandoned all his other business in order to help me. The man made another call and discovered the time George's boat was due and we turned to leave for the docks, but at that moment a well-dressed young man entered the building, carrying a briefcase. Philip called out, 'George!'

The young man turned and smiled at Philip. I did not recognise him at all. The slim boy I remembered had become a tall, well-built man, with a large head, a receding hairline and a dark beard that reminded me rather of Joseph. The man had an assurance, almost a swagger as he strode across the entrance hall, grasped Philip's hand and shook it warmly. Then he turned to me and studied me for a moment, then exclaimed,

'Huw? Is it Huw? Surely...'

Obviously I had changed less than him in the intervening years.

'It's been a long time, George.'

'But...'

He was taking in my smart clothes and my accent. Then he shook my hand, equally warmly. Philip said, 'We were on our way to the docks. The receptionist said you were arriving on the afternoon boat.'

'Something urgent has cropped up in Belfast so I took an earlier boat. I have to speak to the owners. But there's ample time for that. Come up to my office and we can catch up with all our news.'

George's office was large and well furnished, with comfortable chairs as well a drawing board and other apparatus used by an engineer. A secretary brought us coffee and biscuits while George explained why he was spending so much time in Belfast.

'You see, Cunard, our main competitors have stolen a march on us. They've launched a splendid new fleet. You've probably heard of them. Mauretania, Lusitania, etc. Fine ships. Blue Riband candidates for sure. But we are planning our own new fleet. Mr Ismay the Chairman has ordered, and is paying for, three ships. Larger, faster, more comfortable ships than theirs and absolutely unsinkable. That's confidential information by the way.'

He looked at each of us in turn and we both nodded.

'I am involved with the design and that means talking to the shipbuilders over there. They have suggested certain changes in the structure of the hull, so I have to inform my bosses.'

Of course I was interested in George's life but I was impatient to discover more about Amy and the daughter I didn't know I had until last night. Glancing at me Philip seemed to understand my impatience.

'George, I know how important your work is, and we are interested, but Huw came to see you about another matter. You see he has spent the last fifteen years in America. He did not know until last night that Amy was dead or that he had a daughter.'

George rose from his chair and seemed to lose his self-confidence for a moment.

'Oh how selfish of me. Rattling on about my own concerns when...I do apologise. Well, Huw, I will try to answer your questions. Fire away.'

So George told me about the day of his grandmother's funeral. He had been living with Joseph in Liverpool for several years by then, serving his apprenticeship, when news arrived that his grandmother was ill. He hurried to Llanwddyn and stayed with her for a few days. She seemed to get better and was anxious not to disturb his studies, so he returned to Liverpool but a few days later he received a telegram telling him that she had suddenly got worse and died. He went back to the village and arranged the funeral, informing those who would wish to attend, including John Noble and his wife. He knew that Amy would have wanted to attend, but he had absolutely no idea where she was.

'Did no one see her again,' I asked, 'after John sent her away?'

I was surprised when Philip answered.

'Yes, I did. I met her completely by accident in New Brighton, where I had gone for the day as a break from my work at the quarry.'

'How was she?'

'She had matured into a fine looking woman. She was very well dressed, though perhaps a little flashily, and seemed quite happy. At first she was suspicious of my sudden appearance, thinking I had come to pester her again, but eventually things improved between us and we had a most enjoyable day, but all too short.'

'Were you still in love with her?' I asked.

'Oh yes. By the end of that day I certainly was but I had to catch the train back to Machynlleth and return that evening to the quarry. However, I made sure that I had her address, and was determined to see her again.'

'So why..?'

'Well, you see, she had told me a pack of lies and given me a fictitious address. When I wrote to that address my letters were returned. Eventually I went to the place where she had said she was a governess to two young children, but the old couple who answered the door said that they had never had children and told me that unless I stopped bothering them they would inform the police. Thinking that Amy might have mixed up the house numbers I spoke to several neighbours but no-one had ever heard of her. Now...'

Philip paused and I saw tears in his eyes.

'If only I had not rushed back to the quarry that day. If only I had followed her and found out the truth, she might still be alive.'

'So she didn't tell you she had a child?'

'No. I had no idea. I suppose she thought I would be too shocked. And I suppose I would have been if I had known how she was making a living. You remember what a prude I was in the old days. But if she had told me I would still have asked her to marry me and taken her away from that life. After all I had no idea then that you would ever return, and certainly not as a rich man '

All three of us were silent for a while, then George spoke again.

'After the funeral everyone returned to Grandmother's house, where her neighbour and old friend, Mrs Evans- I expect you remember her, Huw- had arranged food and drink for the funeral party. Everyone ate and drank too much and the place soon became very stuffy so Ella and I decided to take a walk beside the lake. We crossed the dam and walked past the straining tower, talking about my grandmother and how she had looked after me since my mother's death, then about the future as my apprenticeship would soon be coming to an end. Soon we reached that place where the river that used to flow through the old village now enters the lake. We saw...'

George stopped for a moment, unable to continue as the sad scene filled his memory again.

'We saw a woman apparently asleep on a small bluff above the lake. A little girl, about four or five years old, sat beside her and as we approached she asked us to wake her mother, because they had to walk on to Bala and catch the train...'

He paused again, his throat constricting and his eyes filling with tears.

'The woman was very thin and her drawn face was very pale. Her clothes were old and ragged, in contrast to the little girl who was well-dressed. Ella knew at once that it was Amy and that she was dying, if not dead already. She sent me off to find help, and took the little girl into her arms...'

I rose from my seat and put my arms around George while he sobbed. When he had regained control of himself, I asked, as if still uncertain of my daughter's existence, 'The little girl? That was my daughter? That was Nan?'

He simply nodded. I helped him back to a seat. We sat in silence for a while, then he continued.

'A post mortem showed that Amy had died from some horrid disease that is common among women of that...'

He could not utter the word.

'When John learned this he was horrified; he would not allow her body to be brought back to his village. He had it announced that Amy had died in another country, which I suppose she had, if Wales is to be thought of as a separate country. She was buried in the new graveyard at Llanwddyn. He did not even attend the service.'

'And Nan?'

'Ella took Nan home with her, in spite of John's protestations. She has lived with John and Ella ever since. John cut off all contact with me, I suppose he thought I might tell people the truth about Amy, but Ella has written to me, in secret, and told me about Nan. In fact I had a letter just before I left for Belfast. I read it on the boat. It's in my pocket now.'

He took the letter out and quoted from it

"She's seventeen now, but not a bit like her mother. Nan is petite and pretty, with dark brown hair and dark brown eyes, which sparkle with intelligence."

George tore off the address from the letter and gave it to me. As I read that address I thought of my daughter living there all these years without me knowing. It was devastating to think that I had missed all those years, when she was growing up. I was determined to see her as soon as possible, but I felt I must pay my respects to poor dead Amy first.

I set off for the Vyrnwy valley that very same day.

Chapter Sixteen

Nan had never travelled on her own before; she was excited but slightly apprehensive. Train travel also felt like a new experience, although she thought she must have travelled with her mother by that means, but so long ago she could not really remember. Now as the train left Shrewsbury and picked up speed she watched the flat fields of north Shropshire scurrying by, full of fat cattle in the meadows and stubble fields left after the harvest. In the distance she could see blue hills rising, which she imagined might be Wales.

She had taken the precaution of getting into a carriage already occupied by two elderly ladies, dressed entirely in black. When she had entered the carriage they had studied her with disapproval, perhaps because she was travelling alone, or simply because she was young and pretty and more colourfully dressed, but they soon became engrossed in their own whispered conversation and forgot she was there.

'It is positively scandalous,' one of them hissed, in an attempt at an upper-class accent. 'The girl was half his age.'

'And he a vicar,' said the other woman, straining to outdo her companion in artificial refinement.

'One might say that he deserved it.'

'I never really liked the man, or his sermons. Far too elaborate for me.'

'Well, one musn't speak too harshly of the dead, I suppose.'

Nan wondered how much harsher you could be, then tried to ignore their conversation and took from her purse the travel instructions that man at the station had given her.

She got off the train at the next station as instructed. The old ladies remained in the carriage, obviously going further north. This station was a junction and one of the porters showed her to the little side platform where her next train, which he called 'The shuttle', waited. This consisted of a small shabby locomotive and a single carriage, which soon set off slowly travelling southwards. Those hills she had seen in the distance approached rapidly, became green rather than blue, and were dotted with sheep.

They soon arrived at another station, which seemed much too large for the little town it served and was surrounded by warehouses and engine sheds and a positive tangle of sidings. Here she had to change trains again, while the little train she had just travelled on made its way back to the last station. Now she understood why it had been called the 'shuttle' It was only a short while before her next train arrived and she was pleased to find an empty carriage but just as the train began to move off a young man opened the door, jumped into the carriage and sat down opposite her, breathing hard as if he had been running.

'Just made it!' he exclaimed, with a little laugh.

Nan felt her face reddening, but after wishing her 'Good Morning' the young man moved circumspectly away from her on the other side of the carriage and took out a newspaper.

Nan smiled shyly and turned to look out of the window, but she had already noted that the young man was dressed in a tweed suit and derby hat and carried a small black case, almost like that of a doctor, though he did not look old enough to be a member of that profession

When the railway left the town it ran parallel with a road and a canal, both busy with traffic. Soon the hill on the right became steep and Nan saw that its sides had been gouged out into a quarry, where mounds of pale grey stone waited to be carried away. Now the line turned westward, along a river valley, where the hills grew higher on either side

and the names of the stations they frequently stopped at became difficult to pronounce, with many 'L's' and 'F's' in the Welsh fashion. Suddenly the young man put down his newspaper and spoke directly to her.

'Look, I mean you no harm, but I cannot help but be curious. I make this journey often, but rarely do I share it with a woman on her own. Especially one so young and pretty.'

Nan blushed. She studied the young man. He had such an open, pleasant face – though not particularly good looking- that she decided his forwardness was simply a way of being friendly.

'Well, you see,' she began, glancing down to make sure that her ring was still in place and the right way round, 'my husband has gone abroad with his regiment and I am looking up a relation I haven't seen for many years'

Well, it wasn't really a lie was it? After all she was on her way to find her mother's grave.

'Ah, I see. Well, I'm on my way to Lake Vyrnwy. I work for the Liverpool Corporation. Every so often I am sent to see that all is well with the lake and the dam.'

Now Nan could not stop herself from saying, 'What a coincidence. I am bound for that lake as well. But I have heard that the train goes no further than Llanfyllin.'

The young man did not sound as if he came from Wales but he said, 'You probably mean (he pronounced the name with a sort of tongue fluttering sound at the beginning, then the 'f' became a 'v' and the 'y' sounded like a 'u'). Don't worry. I only know how to say it because I have been here so many times. Go, on have a go.'

Nan copied his pronunciation and decided that she liked the Welsh way and liked this young man as well. In fact she now trusted him to the extent that she asked, 'So how do you get to the lake from' –she hesitated for a moment then pronounced the name again –' Llanfyllin?'

The young man smiled, 'Excellent. You've already got the idea. Well, you see I have a pony and trap waiting at the station. The corporation books it for me in advance by telephone. You'd be very welcome to share it with me. By the way my name is Trevor. Trevor Jones, which sounds Welsh, but actually I come from Liverpool. I shall be meeting some colleagues in Llanwddyn, which is close to the lake, and making my inspection, then I must return in time to catch the last train so I could bring you back as well. But I suppose you will be staying with your relative.'

'Oh no, this will be a flying visit. Just to re-establish the relationship.'

Nan recognised that she was being devious again but what she said was partly true.

'In that case I'll pick you up from the end of the dam at about half past four. But if you're not there I will have to make my way back to Llanfyllin without you. I dare not miss my train. What's your name by the way?'

'Nan. It's Nan.'

She rarely used her surname. In fact she was not sure which name she should use. She knew that her father's surname was Morris, but her Grandmother was called Noble, and her mother had used yet another name, which she could not at that moment remember.

The young man rose from his seat, walked across the swaying carriage and shook her hand.

'Well, Nan, it's very good to meet you.'

Suddenly the carriage lurched sideways and he was forced to sit down hurriedly opposite her. They both laughed.

The train began to slow as it approached the terminus at Llanfyllin, and soon they were leaving the little town in the pony and trap. The surrounding hills had become even higher now and the road climbed steeply, so that the pony slowed to a walk. Theirs seemed to be the only vehicle on the road this mid-September morning and the only sound was the steady clip, clop of the pony's hooves and bird song from the roadside bushes.

'So, Trevor, what do you actually do when you get to the lake?'

'I meet up with some men who live nearby and look after the lake. We check the condition of the dam, test the purity of the water and make sure that the sluices are working properly.'

'Sluices?'

They release water through the dam so that the river below it continues to flow'

'I see.'

'We also make sure that the straining tower is operating properly.'

Straining tower? There was something familiar about those words. Someone had told her something about them many years ago. Something connected with her mother...

Trevor told her that it was eight miles from Llanfyllin to the lake and so far the road had been uphill most of the way. Now they reached the top of a hill and there below them Nan could see the lake, a long narrow stretch of water, surrounded by wooded hills. From this point the road went mainly downhill and before long they entered a dark wood and when they emerged Nan saw the dam straight ahead of her, a huge wall of grey stone, with little archways across the top.

'What are the little arches for?'

'They carry the road across, like a lot of little bridges joined together, and when the lake is full the water flows over the dam through the arches.'

Trevor explained that he would pick her up at this end of the dam, later in the day, then drove the pony and trap along the road, with the great lake on the right and a deep valley on the left, where a river flowed away from the dam.

At the other end of the dam Trevor helped Nan down from the trap and went on to stable the pony for the day. She stood for a moment looking across the lake, which was very still on this windless day. Then she spotted what she thought must be the straining tower, rising like a fairy tale castle out of the water on the other side of the lake. There was something familiar about that tower; she wondered if she had seen it before. For a moment a chill feeling passed down her spine. The scene was very beautiful and yet she suddenly felt sad. Well, of course, she thought, no wonder I am sad; I am going to see my mother's grave. But first I have to find the church and the graveyard where she is buried.

The village was small, perhaps a dozen houses at most, built of the same grey stone as the dam, and still looking quite new. Of course she remembered her Uncle John telling her that there had been an older village, now submerged beneath the lake, and that those inhabitants who had chosen to remain in the area had been rehoused here in the newly built village. She came to a little shop and went in to ask about the church. At first she thought that the dark interior of the shop was unoccupied, but a voice said, 'Bore da' and when her eyes became accustomed to the gloom she saw a plump little old woman in an apron standing behind the counter.

Nan looked confused.

'Oh, English you are is it? Well good morning to you. What were you wanting?'

'I am looking for the church. A relative of mine is buried in the graveyard.'

'Ah, well you see, wrong side of the dam you are. Those silly men from Liverpool built the village on this side and the church on the other. Quite a walk it is, 'specially when you're getting on a bit. Now, look you, go back over the dam, up the hill a little way, then you'll see a lane going off to the left. There's a sign there tells you. St Wddyn's.'

'Thank you. That's very kind.'

Nan felt that she ought to buy something. She saw some red roses in a bucket near the door.

'I wonder if I may purchase half a dozen of those roses.'

'Course you may. Lovely they are, isn't it. From our own garden. Cut fresh today.'

Nan bought the roses, which the woman wrapped in damp newspaper, thanked her again and left the shop. As she walked back over the dam and looked across to that tower she thought about her father. If that was the straining tower then Ella had told her that the only time she had seen him was outside that tower before he was taken away by the police. What was he like? Had he ever come back to this place? Had he ever tried to contact her mother? Did he know that he had a daughter? If so, why had he never tried to find her? Where was he now?

She felt tears filling her eyes. This place was depressing her. Apart from the shopkeeper she had seen no one. Where were they all?

She reached the end of the dam and began to walk back up the road which had brought her from Llanfyllin. At last she saw a finger post pointing left with a name that looked nothing like the one the shopkeeper had said, but the directions seemed to fit, so she turned left and went up the lane.

It was a warm day, the lane was very steep and soon she had every sympathy with the old shopkeeper, who must make this journey every time she came to a service. Nan hoped that the sermons were worth it.

At last she reached the church, built of that same grey stone. There was a bench near the church door and she sat for a while, getting her breath and taking in the scent of the pines which surrounded the building. She thought about her mother again. They would have brought her here in a coffin and the funeral service would have taken place in this little church. How many mourners would there have been? She guessed very few. She was not even sure that her mother's stepfather had attended. He would never speak of that day. Suddenly a bell rang somewhere above her. It was the clock sounding the time. Two o'clock. Her tears flowed again.

The graveyard was on the other side of the lane. Nan walked along the little paths between the graves and read the names. There was many a Jones and Evans and Williams, two of Davies and a single Edwards. The dates on most of these graves showed that they were relatively new and sadly two of the graves were those of children, one who had lived for only eight days. It was obvious that those buried in these graves were still mourned, because the graves were well tended and vases of flowers were quite fresh.

At the end of the row she came to the grave of a Megan Owen and knew that she had heard that name. She remembered that there was a Harriet Owen buried in the churchyard at Hope Underhill, and that Ella had once explained the connection, but she could not remember what it was. Then suddenly, with a shock of recognition, Nan realised that she had been here before, standing in this exact spot, many years ago, looking at that grave, as a small child, with her mother by her side. There had been no headstone then, just a wooden cross with the name of the deceased, and the mound had been covered in flowers, but she still knew that this is where they had stood.

For a moment Nan felt quite dizzy. A slight breeze had arisen, stirring the surrounding trees. Again she felt that chill pass down her spine.

She moved on quickly to look for her mother's grave. The next row of graves were all of the same kind, and although the grass around them had been trimmed, only one of the graves had flowers on it. But where was her mother's grave?

Nan walked back along the row, but there was no familiar name and the dates, where they had been marked, seemed far too long ago. Then she saw it; one more grave, on its own, in a corner of the graveyard, where the grass had only been roughly cut. Even before she reached the grave she knew that it was her mother's and the name on the stone confirmed it, 'In Memory of Amy, beloved daughter, sister and mother. Taken too soon.'

Now the tears that sprang to Nan's eyes were tears of anger as well as sorrow. Her mother had been buried here, almost hidden in a corner, as if she was to be forgotten as soon as possible. Nan knelt in front of the grave and tore at the grass and weeds which almost obscured the stone until she had created a clear space around it, then she lay down on the soft dry grass, which smelt like new mown hay, and fell asleep.

The church clock woke her, chiming three o'clock. She sat up slowly and looked around. That first hint of breeze she had felt when standing by Megan Owen's grave had become a constant light wind ruffling the tops of the trees and the sky was filled with puffy, fast moving clouds.

Nan remembered the roses. There was no vase on her mother's grave, so she stole one from a better tended grave and looked about for some water. Near the gate into the graveyard was a stand pipe. She guessed that this would have been put in when the Liverpool Corporation built the church and if the water was good enough for the people of Liverpool it was good enough for her, so Amy put her lips to the tap and drank deeply. Then she filled the vase, took it back to the grave and arranged the roses. Again she had a sudden sharp memory from that last time she had been here. She remembered that she and her mother had lifted some flowers from the ones lying on the grave, pretending that they had brought them and laid them back on the grave in a solemn ritual.

She remembered her mother's sad smile and tears came again. Then she remembered that someone had called out to them and they had run away.

Nan knew that she must leave now and walk back to the dam if she was not to miss her lift with Trevor. She wiped her eyes, placed her hand for a moment on her mother's headstone, then walked back towards the gate. As she reached it – one of those kissing gates cleverly designed so that cattle or sheep could not get through – a man appeared. He held the gate open for her, then lifted his hat and wished her good afternoon. His accent was unusual. Not quite Welsh, definitely not English. He was not tall, but he was a handsome man, round about forty she guessed, dressed in expensive looking riding clothes and when he had lifted his riding cap she had seen his dark curly hair, just beginning to grey at the edges. He gave her a friendly smile as she walked through the gate. On the lane she paused for a moment and looked back at the man. He too seemed to be looking for a particular grave and not knowing where it was. But she did not want him to see her spying on him, so she walked on quickly down the lane. There was a horse tethered in the shade. She thought again about the man who had ridden here. But she must hurry now or she would miss her lift back to Llanfyllin.

Chapter Seventeen

The train took me to Bala, where I stayed overnight in the town's best hotel. Next day I bought some riding clothes, hired a horse and set off early in the late September sunshine. I am no great horseman, certainly not in Jed's class, or Philip's, but I remembered how difficult the road was over the mountains between Bala and Vyrnwy and decided that horseback would be the most efficient way to get there.

It was almost midday by the time I reached the valley and saw the lake for the first time. I was astonished by its size and by the way the surrounding valley had been transformed in the intervening years. Thousands of trees had been planted on the hillsides, and a fine road ran alongside the lake. It was almost impossible to recognise where the old village had once been and in fact I did not really recognise anything until the straining tower suddenly appeared. I halted the horse and gazed at that tower which brought back so many memories and mixed feelings of sadness about Amy's death, tenderness as I remembered our lovemaking, and anger about my unjust imprisonment. Then I clicked my tongue and pressed my knees into the horses' flanks until it moved on obediently again.

I was not really sure where the new church was. I remembered blowing up the old church and smiled when I remembered nearly blowing up my father with it. I had been in such a hurry to complete our work and take Amy to our farm that I had been careless with the explosive, but luckily my father had fallen into an open grave and avoided being blown to smithereens. A few nights before, many of the old graves had been dug up so that the coffins could be transferred to the new graveyard. That macabre scene had remained clear in my memory ever since.

When I reached the end of the dam I saw an old man leaning against the parapet, smoking a pipe. He gave me directions to the new church in Welsh, so I set off up the road towards

Llanfyllin as instructed and soon reached the place where a finger post pointed to St Wddyn's Church up a steep lane. I dismounted and walked beside the horse until I reached the church. There was a drinking trough just below the gate into the graveyard. I tethered the horse in the shade, but within reach of the trough, then made for the gate.

Just as I started to open it a young woman appeared on the opposite side. Naturally I held the gate so that she could come through and wished her good morning. I say 'young woman' but she was not much more than a girl, slim and pretty, with dark hair peeping from under a straw bonnet and with deep brown eyes. Her dress was simple but quite colourful. As she passed through the gate I thought her look had sadness about it. She did not return my greeting but merely nodded and hurried on her way. Perhaps, I thought, one of her parents was buried here, perhaps both. But that was none of my business, so I walked on slowly into the graveyard and began to look for Amy's grave.

I soon found the grave where Megan Owen was buried. I thought for a moment of that kind woman whose daughter had been murdered and of the way she had looked after her grandson George ever since. Someone had placed flowers on the grave a few days ago- wallflowers from a cottage garden I suspected- which were just beginning to fade. Perhaps Mrs Evans, her neighbour and friend had brought them when she came to the service on Sunday.

I thought of that fateful day, which George had described, when soon after Mrs Owen's coffin had been lowered into this grave, he and Ella Noble were to discover Amy lying dead beside the lake with our daughter Nan sitting beside her. But Amy was not buried in this part of the graveyard, so I walked on and discovered the graves of those who had been lifted from the old graveyard and reinterred here.

But Amy was not buried in this part of the graveyard either. I began to wonder if George had given me the right information, or perhaps there was another graveyard in another part of the valley. Then I spotted another grave on its own near the edge of the graveyard. I walked over and read the inscription, 'My beloved Amy. Taken too soon.'

I fell to my knees and tears sprang to my eyes. I remembered Amy as she had been when we met here in this valley so many years ago. She was tall, almost as tall as me, slim but shapely with an erect posture. Her face was striking, rather than merely pretty, with high cheek bones, a straight nose, large green eyes and a well-shaped lips that were usually slightly curled in an enigmatic smile. Her hair was a rich gold but in certain lights it had reddish tints. No wonder all the men who met her during her brief stay in the Vyrnwy valley were immediately captivated; Phillip, George, myself of course, and even Joseph, Philip's father.

How could that lovely young girl, who had held me close, and let me take her virginity, be lying under this earth, her body rotting away? And why was she buried on her own in a corner of the graveyard, as if despised? Yet not entirely despised because someone had visited this grave very recently, had pulled away the weeds and long grass with their bare hands, leaving the torn tussocks in a pile beside the grave. Whoever it was had also placed a splendid bunch of red roses in a vase on top of the grave. Surely those were not the sort of flowers the likes of Mrs Evan would place on the grave of someone she had met briefly, so many years ago. I could not imagine Ella travelling all the way from that village in England to tend her daughter's grave, even if her husband had allowed her to come. It certainly wouldn't have been her husband, who had not even attended his step-daughter's funeral.

I sat on the dry turf and thought for a while. Then suddenly it came to me. I remembered George quoting from a letter Ella had sent him.

'She is seventeen now, but not a bit like her mother. She is very petite and pretty, with dark brown hair and dark brown eyes, which sparkle with intelligence.'

Of course! I had just seen my daughter, wished her good morning and let her go on her way. I did not know why she had chosen this particular time to visit her mother's grave. Perhaps she came here often?

I rose rapidly, put my hand on the cold headstone of Amy's grave and hoped that she was in a better place, though I did not really believe it, then hurried to the gate. I was in such a state by now, almost of panic, that I tried to open the gate the wrong way and the more I pushed on the swinging section the more firmly it stayed shut. Then I recovered my senses and opened it the right way. My horse, still steaming slightly from its earlier exertions was reluctant to move out of the shade, but at last I turned it round and jumped into the saddle. Soon I realised that the lane was too steep to make the horse do more than walk and even then its shoes slipped slightly on the metalled surface, but at last I reached the dam. The man with the pipe had gone. I urged my mount into a trot and crossed the dam. In the village I found a small shop and entered. The shopkeeper told me, in Welsh that, yes, she had seen a young woman such as I described, but much earlier in the day. The shopkeeper had never seen her before. She had asked where the graveyard was and bought some red roses for her mother's grave.

I muttered, 'Diolch' and 'Hwyl' and almost ran from the shop. I paused at the near end of the dam. Here a road ran along this side of the lake. But if she was on foot Nan would not have gone that way. There was nowhere she could have come from, which was served by the railway, except Llanwcllyn on the far side of the Cambrian Mountains, and that was a long lonely road. I re-crossed the dam and stopped at the other end to look down the road which I had ridden along that morning. That led to Bala, where she might have got off the train, but that too was a long, long walk and unless she had left very, very early in the morning I would surely have passed her on the way.

At last the most obvious answer came to me. Llanfyllin! George had told me that the village where the Nobles lived was a few miles south of Shrewsbury. So Nan, and I was now convinced that it was Nan, would have travelled from Shrewsbury to Llanfyllin which was by several miles the closest station to Llanwddyn.

I thought for a moment of riding on towards Llanfyllin, hoping to catch up with Nan, but my horse was already tired and I still had to ride back to Bala. No, the sensible thing was to spend the night at the splendid hotel which had been built on the hillside overlooking the lake, telephone the stables in Bala and tell them I would bring the horse back next day. After that I would return to Liverpool, collect a change of clothes and make my way to Shrewsbury, find that village, what was it called, 'Hope something'? Ah yes, 'Hope Underhill,' where I had been told my daughter lived.

Chapter Eighteen

The long hot summer had come to an abrupt end on the previous Sunday so that as Nan made her way to the Infirmary for her second day as a hospital volunteer rain was falling heavily from a gloomy sky and rivulets were rushing down the gutters on both sides of Castle Hill. The wheels of heavily laden carts and the occasional lorry were spraying unwary pedestrians and the long skirts of the day were soon soaked around the hem. She had told her landlady that her volunteering had begun but she did not tell her where it was happening or how soon it was to become a proper training. She was still fearful that her stepfather would discover where she was and drag her back to Hope Underhill, though she did wonder why he would bother.

Yesterday she had met the formidable Sister Gaunt – by name and nature thought Nan- and been told very clearly what she may do or not do. Nothing that Nan would have called nursing was allowed. She could speak to the patients and pass on their requests to the nurses – bed pans, drinks, etc. – and she could give comfort to those who needed it, and there many of those, because this was a Children's Ward. She was surprised to discover that the boy with the broken leg had already gone home.

'Good job, too,' said Gaunt, 'A thief and a liar and a trouble-maker too!'

'Did he leave an address?'

'That's not for you to know. And even if he did he probably made it up. Gave us a different name every day'

'How will he manage with his leg in plaster? Had he learned to use a crutch?'

'Oh, yes. He was soon dashing about like anything. He tripped up one nurse with it and threatened to use it on the back-side of another.'

Nan just managed to suppress a giggle and muttered, 'How dreadful!' instead.

'I told him that I was informing the matron of his behaviour. He had seen the matron. She's a formidable lady. So he discharged himself, well, not officially, he simply left and took the crutch with him, which is of course hospital property. Now, that's quite enough chatter, Mrs Brown. Please continue with your duties.'

Nan muttered 'Yes, Ma'am' and gave a slight curtsey before walking away. She would have to find another way of discovering the boy's address. After all, Gaunt seemed to be an excellent nurse and there was no point in making an enemy of someone who might soon be supervising her probation, if and when she was taken on.

She had been asked to supply two references. She had written immediately to Robert Moreton and her friend Jane Meredith, a friend of her grandmother's, explaining what she needed and asking them not to tell anyone about her application to become a probationer or to give anyone her new address and to use her adopted name. Both had replied immediately and told her that they would be sending testimonials to the hospital as soon as possible. She hoped that the hospital would not insist on references from her school, but perhaps they would be so impressed by receiving one from Squire Moreton that they would not pursue that line of enquiry.

As she turned to the other little patients in their beds she thought again about that boy. He seemed to have lived on his wits and his nimbleness, so how would he manage now? She was wondering how she could find his address when she heard a pathetic voice calling from one of the beds.

'Nurse...Nurse!'

The children did not distinguish nurse from volunteer, so long as someone cared. She went over to the bed where Agnes lay, so small and thin that she hardly made any mound in the bedclothes, and bent over her flushed face.

'What is it, Agnes?'

'Thirsty. Very thirsty.'

Nan had been told that the little girl had severe pneumonia and was not likely to survive. She had been brought into the hospital because her mother had ten other children and could not cope, especially as her husband was working away somewhere.

Nan looked around for a nurse, but there was only Gaunt, standing near her office, apparently watching her. She made the gesture of drinking and Gaunt nodded and gave what might have been the slightest smile. As she went to fetch a drink for Agnes she thought that perhaps Gaunt was not such a bad old stick after all.

Walking back to Agnes's bed she saw a young nurse enter at the other end of the ward and was pleased to see that it was Sarah Heath, a plumply pretty and good natured young woman, who was in her third year of training. She had been given responsibility for Nan when she began her volunteering yesterday and they had hit it off immediately. Some of the other nurses, who were generally much older, seemed almost to resent Nan's presence and were unwilling to answer her questions about the patients, saying that they didn't have time for 'chit-chat'. Now Sarah told her which patients she should attend to and they shared some brief conversations when Gaunt was not around.

'Do you remember the boy with the broken leg, Sarah.'

'Of course. He was a card, that one.'

'Do you know where he lives?'

'Oh yes. I remember writing it down for our records. Why?'

'It was me who saw his accident and brought him into the infirmary. I'd just like to know how's he's getting on.'

'Well I wouldn't advise you to go down there. King's Head Passage is in one of the worst parts of the town.'

'Oh!'

'Yes. Off Mardol, just by the King's Head. Definitely not a place for the likes of us to go, specially not at night.'

'I see.'

'Now you see Peter, in that end bed. Been here for ages. Got bed sores. Needs lifting and turning. We'll need to work together.'

As they dealt with Peter, Nan rehearsed that address in her head. Perhaps she was naive, or just very stubborn, but she had already decided that she would visit King's Head Passage that very night.

It had rained again so that when Nan made her way down the street called Mardol, which led to the river and the Welsh Bridge there were deep puddles everywhere and she had to tread carefully in the gloom. A chill in the air made it seem later in the year than the last days of September. The shops were still open though very few shoppers were about but as she walked down towards the Kings Head she saw a number of women, some quite old, some very young, leaning against the walls, as if waiting for someone. She was wearing a cloak against further rain but as she lifted it to check where she was, one of these women scowled and muttered, 'Shift yourself, young 'un. This is my pitch.'

At last she reached the tavern and looked down the narrow unlit passage beside it. She almost fell over a man huddled against the wall with one leg stretched out on the pavement, a badly written notice leaning against the stump where his other leg should have been, and a flat cap holding a single copper coin. The message read, 'Boer War Vetran –lost me leg in the Transval'

Nan leant forward, placed another coin in the cap and asked, 'I wonder if you could help me. I'm looking for a boy about ten years old. He has a broken leg.'

'Lucky ain't 'e. Least it'll mend.'

'I'm not sure of his name.'

'Oh yes, I think I know who you means. Old Ma Dorricott's lad. Why would you be lookin' fer 'im? Pinched summat of yourn 'as 'e?'

'Oh no, I was there when he was injured. I just wanted to see how he was getting on. Do you know where he lives?'

'I might and I might not'

The man lifted the greasy cap and shook it so that the few coins in it clinked together. Nan got the message, took another coin from her purse and placed it in the cap.

The man put the cap down again and took something out of his jacket pocket. The light of a match suddenly flared in Nan's face.

'My, you'm a pretty 'un. You oughtn't stay be round 'ere. 'Aint safe.'

'I just want to know where he lives, that's all.'

He pointed along the passage.

'Down there. King's Head Passage. Number eight. Got a blue door. Now get going'

Nan thanked the man and turned to go, but just then a large man came stumbling out of the pub and put his arm around her. He stank of drink and he held on tight to her arm as if to hold himself up. He pulled back her cloak and lifted up her chin.

'Well, well. What 'ave we here. Now there's rare sight in this neck of the woods. Youth. Beauty. And innocence I guess. Now I reckon you're just what I'm looking for...'

Nan tried to get away but the man's grip was strong. She was petrified, but just then the veteran on the pavement leant over and pulled the man's leg so that he toppled forward.

'Now run...'

The large man had loosed her arm to stop himself falling so Nan dashed down the passage. She heard the drunken man swearing at the old soldier on the ground and knew that he was in real trouble but he had saved her and she was grateful for that. By now her eyes had become accustomed to the gloom in the passage and she counted the doors of the hovels along its length. She saw what might have been a blue door, though the paint was faded and blistered and there was no number to be seen. She hesitated, then heard that horrible man lumbering down the passage behind her, so she knocked on the door, walked in and closed the door behind her.

She found herself in a cold room, lit by just one candle. There was an old woman lying on a bed in one corner, moaning. No fire in the grate. The boy held a cup of something to the old woman's lips. He put the cup down and turned to Nan.

'What you doing here?'

'I came to see how you were.'

The boy was obviously embarrassed to be seen in this hovel.

'Well you've seen. Now you can go.'

The old woman peered at Nan.

'Who's this Jim?'

So that was his name.

'Just a busybody from up the 'ospital Gran'

When Nan looked closer she could see how thin the old woman was. She asked her, 'When did you last have something to eat?'

The old woman croaked, 'Day afore yesterday. Jim brought some bread and cheese. He's a good lad. But he can't get about so good with his leg like that.'

Nan smiled to herself thinking that was because he'd get caught stealing now. She lifted the cup from which the old woman had been drinking and sniffed, 'What's in this?'

'Drop of gin. Gives her comfort.'

'Look,' said Nan, 'I've got a few shillings. Let me go and get some food. I'm hungry too. Then perhaps we can get that fire going. What d'you think, Jim?'

The thought of food and warmth overcame the boy's shame. He nodded. Nan left, hurrying down the passageway, but keeping an eye out for that drunken man.

Shops were open late in this neighbourhood, so Nan quickly purchased some bread and ham, and a packet of tea. Then she saw some firewood and bought that too.

Luckily there was nobody about as she hurried back to the blue door, but when she opened it a man stood swaying beside the boy. He held a leather belt in his hand.

'Who the 'ell?'

Nan put her purchases on the table and felt for her purse.

'I helped your son the other day when he was run over. I came to see how he was. '

'You're one of them bloody do-gooders, ain't yer. Well, you can bugger off. This lad of mine's supposed to look after his old dad. But he goes and gets his leg broke.'

He lifted the belt ready to strike Jim. Nan took the last few coins out of her purse.

'Here you are. It's all I have. But it should buy you a few drinks.'

The man looked at the money, then at the boy. At last his thirst overcame his desire to inflict pain. He took the money, fixed his belt back on and stumbled to the door. His lips curled around black teeth as he hissed.

'Make sure you aint 'ere when I gets back.'

When he'd gone Jim came to Nan and hugged her. She broke away.

'Quick let's get the fire lit. You have matches?'

Jim reached up to the mantelpiece and brought down a box of safety matches.

'Some old geezer left these on a bench when he'd lit his pipe.'

While Jim laid the fire and got it going, Nan cut the bread and made ham sandwiches. Soon the kettle was boiling and she made black tea.

The old woman dipped her sandwich in her tea to soften it for her toothless gums. Jim ate his sandwich slowly, savouring every piece. Nan didn't eat. She would get something back at her lodgings.

Soon the food in her stomach and the heat from the fire sent the old woman to sleep. Nan asked, 'Is this your grandmother, Jim?'

'Yea, she's looked after me since my Mum died. But she's old now and I look after her, but since my leg got broke...'

Jim spread some blankets on the floor in front of the fire. He lay down muttering, 'Thanks Nan.'

It wasn't long before he was asleep as well.

Nan buttoned her coat to the neck and tip-toed out of the room. She hurried back to her lodgings, thinking all the way how Ella had looked after her, since *her* mother died. Tomorrow she must go to Hope Underhill and see how Ella was getting on. Her stepfather would be at the school so they could have a good chat.

As she walked beside Shrewsbury Gaol on her way back to her lodgings Nan began to think about men. Jim's dad was obviously a cruel man but so was John Noble because according to her Uncle John he had caused the death of his step-daughter. And her own father had apparently abandoned her. Bloody men!

Next day was Friday and Nan finished her volunteering duties at lunchtime. She borrowed Sarah's bicycle, promising to return it that evening, and set off for Hope Underhill. It was quite a slog climbing out of Shrewsbury but she was young and fit and at last the road began to descend into the green valley between the Long Hill on the left and the jagged ridge of the Devil's Peak on the right. She reached the village just as the church clock struck two so she knew she would have more than an hour to spend with her grand-mother before John closed the school.

Ella greeted her with a firm hug and tears in her eyes. Then she made tea and they sat at the kitchen table to swap their news. Nan wrote her new address on a slip of paper, which Ella folded and placed in her apron pocket. Her tears began again as Ella bemoaned the fact that she had now lost her son and her granddaughter.

'Oh no, Granny, I'm only a few miles away and I'll visit often, when Mr Noble's at school. And Uncle John has gone on a great adventure. Think of all the stories he'll have to tell when he comes back.'

'But will he ever come back. He hates his father so much.'

'Oh time will heal, I'm sure. And now you know my address you can come and visit me.'

'Well, I'll try. But you know how much I hate leaving the village.'

Nan explained about her volunteering at the Infirmary and her hope soon to become a trainee nurse.

'I'm sure you'll do very well. I'm quite jealous of you and John setting out on life's journey, while I...'

Nan took her grandmother's hands in her hers, suddenly noting how old they had begun to look, with raised veins and liver spots. They drank their tea and shared village gossip until the clock in the kitchen showed a quarter past three.

'You'd better leave now, my dear,' said Ella. He sometimes closes the school a little earlier on a Friday, as you know.'

Ella came to the door to see her granddaughter off, and Nan thought how desolate she looked standing there watching her cycle away. The clouds were gathering again and Ella suspected that Nan was going to get wet before she got home.

A few minutes later John came home from school. He saw a young woman cycling towards the Shrewsbury Road. She looked familiar and he guessed what had happened. When he reached the door he saw a small piece of paper lying on the doorstep. He hated litter so he put it in his pocket before setting off for his customary walk up the Long Hill.

Later that night Ella felt in her apron pocket for the slip of paper with Nan's address, but it had gone.

When Nan woke next morning her room was full of light. The recent rain seemed to have washed the sky clean and she could hear the river tumbling heavily over the weir. It was already early October but it promised to be a lovely day. She had just got out of bed and put on her dressing gown when there was a light tap on her door and Sarah came rushing in.

'Oh, Nan, I have some splendid news.'

Sarah's face was alight with the pleasure of imparting her good tidings.

'Well,' said Nan. 'It must be very good news to bring you here so early.

'Oh, I always wake early on my day off. And anyway it's not that early. You must have slept well after all your exercise yesterday.'

At that moment the clock of a nearby church began to chime the hour of nine. They both laughed.

'Come on then. What's this news?'

'One of the students about to begin training has dropped out. Matron said you were next on the list. She asked me to say you could start on Monday.'

'That's wonderful. I've enjoyed the volunteering, but to be properly trained...'

'Right, let's celebrate by having a good walk. It's a lovely day. I suggest the riverside path and then up Haughmond Hill. We'll take picnic.'

Sarah had brought a rucksack. They bought rolls and ham and lemonade and set off.

Soon they left the riverside and took the road towards the hill, passing the sign to the village of Uffington. It was midday by the time they reached the top and sat on a rock that had dried in the sun and looked at the town spread out beneath them. It's brick tentacles were spreading rapidly across the meadows.

Sarah had completed her first year of training. She explained to Nan that nursing could be hard at times and unpleasant, especially when a patient you had got to know suddenly died, particularly if it was a child.

When they had finished their meal they sat talking and listening to the birds in the trees. In mid-afternoon the air suddenly became chill and they decided to walk back.

Mrs Burton met them at the door.

'Oh, Mrs Brown, you've just missed your visitor.'

'Who?'

'He wouldn't give his name. And he asked for a Miss Williams. He didn't know you were married now.'

'What did he look like?

'He was tall and thin. Well spoken. Smartly dressed. But he didn't look too well. And he seemed rather bad-tempered. Especially when I told him your married name. He asked me to describe you. When I told him you were of small stature and dark of hair and eye, he muttered something like, 'That's her, the little slut'. That made me angry and I told him to go. He said he would come back tomorrow.'

'I see. I can't think who that could be. But thank you for letting me know'

She took Sarah up to her room.

'That was almost certainly my step-father. I don't know how he got my address. I certainly don't want to see him.

'Well you'd be entitled to live in the Students' Quarters from tomorrow.'

'What time are you back on the Ward?'

'At Noon'

'Well come here at about ten o'clock in the morning. The Burton's attend chapel then. You can help me move. I don't have much to carry. Uncle John gave the Burton's a month's rent in advance, so they won't miss out. Will you help me?'

'Of course,' said Sarah with a smile.' It sounds fun.'

Chapter Nineteen

Hope Underhill was just as Amy had described it all those years ago. Aptly named, it lay in a narrow valley tucked between two ranges of hills. It had taken me a couple of hours to walk here from Shrewsbury so I was glad to find an inn and slake my thirst, thankful that I was no longer in Wales where such an establishment would be firmly closed on the Lord's Day.

I was directed to the school house by the landlord.

'Tis right beside the church, next the school itself. You'll find that John Noble a dour fellow. Been the Master 'ere for a lifetime. Taught me many years ago, or tried to. '

I thanked him and went on my way. The village itself was a quarter of a mile or so along a narrow lane.

When I knocked at the schoolhouse door, the man himself opened it. I was quite shocked at how he had aged, but he recognised me straight away. His face turned purple and he growled.

'If you are who I think you are then you've got a damned cheek coming here. If I were a younger man I'd knock you to the ground.'

I ignored this, knowing that I could floor this bag of bones with one blow, should it come to that.

'I've come to see my daughter.'

'She doesn't live here anymore.'

'Are you sure? I've come a long way to see her.'

'I thought you were dead.'

'You hoped I was.'

A flicker of a smile crossed the man's face.

'But you and your wife have looked after her all these years. Why should you want to be rid of her now?'

'Because she's a liar, using my name and pretending a status she doesn't have. She may also be a thief, because I don't know how she can manage to keep herself, unless she's stolen from me without me knowing, or perhaps she is prepared to sell herself...'

Now I was barely able to stop myself from hitting him. Was this really the same man who had stayed in my home when he was suffering from that unpleasant ailment while Amy, Philip and I climbed Cadair Idris? Was this the man who seemed at that time to care so much for Amy, his step-daughter?

But then my attitude softened. After all this was the man who had given my daughter a home, had fed and clothed her since she was a little girl. Which was a damn sight more than I had ever done! So what had now caused such a rift between the man and girl?

I had never met Amy's mother but George had a very high opinion of her. Perhaps if I could talk to her?

John Noble stood in the doorway, glaring at me still.

'Is your wife at home?' I asked.

'No, she is not.'

I decided there was no point in continuing this exchange, so I turned away. The man shouted after me.

'I will tell you where your daughter is...'

I turned back.

'So long as you promise to take her far away from me. I never want to see her again.'

He handed me a small piece of paper, went into his house and shut the door.

I stood for a moment, astonished at this turn of events. Glancing at the paper I saw an address in Shrewsbury. Perhaps this was a trick simply to get rid of me. But if it was true I was within a good walk of seeing the daughter I had never known. I set off back to Shrewsbury at a good pace.

By the time I got back to the small hotel where I had stayed the previous night I was footsore and very hungry. After a simple but satisfying meal I sat in the little parlour and fell asleep in my chair. When I woke again it was almost dark. Far too late to go disturbing

anyone, daughter or not, even if I could get my legs going again.

Next morning I asked the hotel landlady where I could find the address written on the piece of paper. She wasn't sure but thought it must be somewhere near the prison. Hmm, that didn't sound too promising, but I set off nevertheless. Outside the railway station a helpful porter loading luggage into a cab explained to me that I must cross the footbridge which went right over the station and that I would then be facing the prison entrance and if I went down the hill on the right I would come to the street I wanted.

I followed the prison walls down the hill. The district was much pleasanter than I had expected and the houses on the right had a fine view of the river.

'Mrs Burton?'

'Yes'

'I've come to see a young lodger of yours. Miss Williams.'

'Who?'

'Nan Williams.'

'I don't have a lodger of that name.'

I was puzzled.

'I did have a young lodger. A Mrs Brown.'

Now something John Noble had said about Nan claiming an undeserved status made sense.

'But she's gone. Did a flit. Taken her things and gone.'

'Gone where?'

'I have no idea. Was she a relative of yours?'

'Yes. My daughter.'

'Your daughter! Yet you didn't know she was married.'

'It's a long story.'

'I can see you've had a shock. You've gone quite pale. Come in and have a cup of tea.'

'No thank you. I must get on. This Mrs Brown, what did she look like?'

'Oh, very young, very pretty and, I thought, very happy. That's why it was such a surprise when she suddenly left.'

'Thank you for your time, Mrs Burton. Oh by the way, did she owe you any rent?'

'No, her husband paid in advance. Before he left.'

'Left?'

'To join his regiment. That's why she was staying here.'

I was more puzzled than ever.

'Well I do hope you find her,' said Mrs Burton. 'Such a pretty little thing'.

Next morning I went to the offices of the Shrewsbury Chronicle and asked for an entry to be placed in the Personal Column of the next edition.

"Would Nan Williams, or Mrs Nan Brown, write to the Adelphi Hotel, Ranelagh Street, Liverpool where she will learn something to her advantage. Letters should be addressed to Mr H. Morris, showing clearly the senders address."

The entry was to be printed in such a way that it would be easily noticed.

Today was Monday and the next edition would not be published until Friday, so I caught the next train to Liverpool.

Chapter Twenty

By midday on Saturday Nan was exhausted. It had been a long hard week. A mixture of lectures and practical work from eight in the morning, sometimes to nine at night. She had learned some basic anatomy, omitting those parts of the body that were not deemed suitable for such young minds, although Nan had learned about them in the playground long ago. She had been taught how to clean a wound and bandage it up. In pairs they had learned how to lift a patient without injuring the patient or themselves. She had been given one free afternoon and her week ended today at 1 o'clock until early Morning on Monday.

She had found the other students friendly enough but had been too tired to socialise and the discipline was fierce. She had heard one of the older students say, 'We might as well be nuns'

The food was tolerable and the beds narrow and hard, but by the end of the day Nan felt she could have slept on the floor.

Her testimonials had been acceptable, especially that from Robert Moreton. She was generally liked by the qualified nurses and managed not to raise the wrath of the terrifying matron during their occasional meetings as she inspected the wards.

Nan was sitting on her bed recovering from her first week when her friend Sarah rushed into their dormitory clutching a newspaper. Sarah had already been training for six months and was well advanced of Nan so they rarely met during training sessions

'I've been trying to catch you all morning. I found this copy of yesterday's Advertiser left on somebody's bed. There's something you ought to see in the personal column"

Nan read the piece from Huw and became very excited. Her father wanted her to contact him. For the first time in her life she would be meeting him. She wondered what he would be like.

'Oh Sarah. It's wonderful news. Thank you so much for showing me. I'll write to him straight away.

Nan had a few sheets of notepaper and two envelopes in her bedside locker, so in a few minutes the job was done.

The two of them quickly checked their clothes and their light make up-nothing more noticeable was allowed-and set out for the Post Office which was only a street away. But when Nan and Sarah reached St Mary's Street they were astonished to find crowds filling the pavements and chattering excitedly. The Post Office was just opposite but when they started to cross the street there were three loud bangs on a drum and a brass band came swiftly towards them. The musicians broke into the familiar tune about the conquering hero coming and the girls decided to let them go past before crossing the street, but after the band had gone by the crowd followed and Nan and Sarah were forced to go with them.

The crowd followed the band down St Mary's Street and turned right into High Street and at last they reached the Market Square where the band stopped and formed up to entertain the crowd.

Sarah asked Nan, 'Any idea what this is all about?

Nan shook her head.

At that moment a young boy approached and thrust a handbill into Sarah's hand. She unfolded it and exclaimed, 'Oh, I see. Look Nan.' Nan saw that the handbill was advertising a circus which was due to perform in the park that evening. She'd love to go but the cost of entry was quite expensive, so she shook her head reluctantly.

Just then a tall, thin young man stood beside them and asked,

'Not going then? What's the problem? Cash?'

Nan blushed and tried to move away, but Sarah was older and more experienced. She often flirted a little with young men but never went too far. The young man persisted. He was accompanied by another young man, shorter and stouter, but with a friendly smile, who seemed to attach himself to Nan.

'We don't have that kind of money. We haven't qualified as nurses yet.'

Nan studied these young men while Sarah spoke and saw that they were dressed simply but neatly. They were well mannered and seemed respectable. She quite liked the shorter one with his friendly smile. But she thought about how John Noble would react if he saw her chatting to a strange man in the street, but John had no hold over her now.

The taller one spoke again. 'My name is Ralph. My friend is Norman. Have you had any lunch, ladies? Norman and I have just been given a bonus. We'd love to treat you.'

Sarah looked doubtful but Nan had missed lunch and her stomach suddenly rumbled. 'That would be lovely. Nothing too expensive, mind.'

'The Black Horse does splendid meals for half a crown.'

So to the Black Horse they went, and Sarah relaxed a little. The young men explained that they were civil servants and had received a bonus for completing some particularly difficult forms.

Nan ordered a meat pie and Sarah plaice and chips. The young men also chose the pie and drank pints of ale. The girls stuck to lemonade.

The conversation became more convivial. The girls gave their names and asked for details of the young men's work and the girl's nursing duties were exchanged.

After a very pleasant hour or so the young men explained that they had to leave as they were going to watch a football match between Shrewsbury Town and Wellington Town at the Barrack's Ground, but if the ladies still wanted to visit the circus, they could meet up at the entrance to the big top at seven o'clock. Nan and Sarah agreed.

By now it was mid-afternoon so the girls decided to walk to the park and relax beside the river, rather than return to the Nurses' quarters. Although it was mid-October the weather was quite pleasant still and it would be light enough till 6 o'clock. They talked about the two young men who had treated them to lunch and decided that they were very kind and polite. They decided that it would be quite safe to help them spend that bonus, so they decided they would meet them at seven o'clock.

The girls walked down towards the river and inspected the circus tent, which was very big indeed. It was difficult to imagine how it had been erected so quickly and would have to be taken down again after the show tonight, as the circus would be moving on to Chester. Sarah and Nan then continued walking along the river bank. The river almost encircled the town, and the walkway was shaded by trees. They looked up at the famous school on the hill across the river and saw some of the pupils taking boats from the boathouse and rowing up river.

By the time they had followed the river as far as the English Bridge and stopped for a cup of tea in a little café at the bottom of Wyle Cop, the light was fading and it was time to retrace their steps towards the big top. When they reached the tent they saw the young men coming towards them from the opposite direction. The first thing that worried them was their unsteadiness and their flushed faces. Sarah whispered to Nan, 'They've been drinking!'

Ralph immediately took Sarah by the arm and went to the box office. Norman offered his arm but Nan refused. She did not like the sickly leer that had replaced his friendly smile. He went to get their tickets but soon turned and said to Nan, 'I'm two bob short. Can you help me out.' She thought of walking away but she really wanted to see the show so she searched her purse and gave him her last two shillings.

The seats were close together and Nan felt Norman's body close to her and what was worse she smelled the alcohol on his breath. But when the show began, she forgot all that in her delight at the colour and life in the ring. First the imposing figure of the ringmaster, who swirled and cracked his whip which brought a line of white horses prancing in and round the ring, lifting their hooves to the rhythm of the music. Nan only knew the wild ponies on the long Hill or the steady beasts who pulled the carts or carriages for people in the village, but these well trained, beautiful animals were quite different. Next it was clowns who tumbled and threw buckets of water at each other and had the audience roaring with laughter. The other acts that followed were equally magical and Nan was engrossed until she felt a warm hand feeling under her skirts. That was too much. She leapt up, stumbled down the steps to the ground and left the tent. Sarah didn't seem to have noticed, so Nan hurried along the dark paths until she reached the well-lit streets. Most of the shops were closed and when she got to the Post Office she read that the last collection that day had gone.

There were tears in her eyes as she brought out the crumpled, forgotten letter from her pocket. She had no stamp, it was too late to go bothering the other nurses and students, and anyway no more letters would be going today.

Chapter Twenty One

No letter had arrived from Nan by Sunday morning. Had she even seen my advert in the Advertiser? Did she ever read the local newspaper? Oh well, I would do the other thing I had planned and hope a letter would arrive in the afternoon post.

'I am expecting a very important letter' I said to the receptionist. 'It will be post-marked Shrewsbury. Please let me know as soon as it arrives. But I shall be out most of today, and I might not be back this evening'

'Very well, Mr Morris. If it arrives the letter will be put in your pigeon hole.'

So I gave the man a shilling which I had learned was the right amount. It still tickled me to think that I could so easily please people, such as I used to be, with a small piece of silver.

'By the way, how do I get to Dollgellau?'

'Well, that's rather a complicated route.' He got out his Bradshaws and looked up Dolgellau. 'You take the train to Chester, then change to the Shrewsbury train and change at Ruabon. But you may have to wait some time for a train to Dolgellau. After all it is Sunday and it's not the holiday season, so the trains are less frequent.'

'Thank you,' I said, and proffered another shilling, which disappeared into the Receptionist's top pocket.

'Thank you Mr Morris.' The man practically bowed. I felt rather embarrassed, in fact, a bit of a fraud, so I quickly made my way to the station.

It was mid-afternoon by the time I reached Dolgellau. My plan was to walk to my old home at Ty Craig, which I hadn't seen for almost twenty years. At first it was pleasant to rediscover so many sights I remembered as I climbed the steep hill from the town, the mountains rising around me, especially Cadair Idris firmly placed on my right, bringing back so many memories of that climb with Amy and Phillip all those years ago.

I was getting warm with the climb in the Autumn sunshine but when I reached the top of the pass the weather changed abruptly and the valley below me was in shadow. I noticed as I descended that my legs were not as strong as they used to be, and the last few yards of my walk ended as a plod. At last I reached the turning to our little farm and was filled with a sense of desolation. Everything looked unused, derelict, empty. There was no sound of any living animal or human. Fences were broken and the fields were filled with weeds.

When I reached the house, the door was locked and someone had fixed pieces of wood across the door. I gathered some tools from the shed and removed the wood. Then I hammered at the lock until it broke. Inside it was as if no one had ever lived here, but I could clearly remember my da sitting in the kitchen smoking his pipe and Nan's strange chatter as she worked. My eyes filled with tears.

I knew what had happened to my father. Phillip had told me about the accident on the little railway that took the slate down to Machynlleth, but my sister had just disappeared. Then I noticed a letter on the kitchen table almost lost in dust. I blew the dust off and saw my name on the envelope, almost faded away.

In the letter Nan explained that she had waited, hoping to hear from me, but no one seemed to know where I had gone, or could be bothered to tell her, so eventually she had to sell the animals, and go to stay with a cousin in South Wales. More tears flowed, then I wiped them away and sighed with relief. At least my little sister had found a safe haven, in where was it? Merthyr Tydfil.

By the time I walked back to Dolgellau it was dark and the last train had gone, so I booked into a hotel, then walked the streets looking for a place to eat. When I sat down in the only restaurant that was still open, I discovered a newspaper left on the seat by a recent customer. On the back page was a list of properties for sale. One of these caught my eye.

'Ty Craig. A small holding, situated between Dolgellau and Machynlleth, abandoned by its previous tenants. In need of complete repair and restocking. Accommodation for small family, To let or for sale. Interested parties should contact M. Williams and Sons, Land agents. Manchester.

I knew at once where my future lay and hoped that no one had beaten me to it. I also hoped that both the Nan's could be persuaded to join me in the adventure.

I caught an early train next morning and was back in Liverpool by lunchtime. There was a letter waiting for me in my pigeon hole. I took it into the lounge and tore it open. Yes, it was from my daughter Nan. She explained that she had become a student nurse and was living at the Nurse's quarters. Her duties kept her busy most days until late but they finished at 12.30 on Saturday, so we could meet up then. She was delighted to hear from me and very excited to be meeting me soon.

I really wanted to rush off to Shrewsbury then and there, but I realised that it would be difficult for Nan, and then I remembered that I had promised to assist Phillip that afternoon at his final meeting before the election. The meeting was due to begin at 2pm.

I hurried to the hall. There was no sign of that ugly mob who had interrupted the meeting last time, and there was more presence of the police. Perhaps Phillip was getting more respect. Or was it simply that an afternoon meeting meant that the crowd had had less time to take on alcohol. I noticed to my surprise that there were more women in the audience, some with children clinging to their skirts.

When Phillip appeared he was warmly welcomed and his speech went down well, except for his support for women's suffrage which again raised hackles and growls among the largely male crowd. But at the end of the speech there was none of that animosity that brought the last meeting to a raucous end. I was glad of that because my body still felt sore in places.

I went quickly backstage to congratulate the speaker and to tell him about my return to Ty Craig and that my daughter had contacted me. He was delighted by this news and asked when that was going to happen. I explained about her nursing duties and that Saturday seemed the most likely time. Phillip looked at me with a wry smile and said, 'That doesn't sound like Huw Morris. He usually wants things to happen immediately. I certainly think you should go and buy the farm at once, and meet Nan as soon as possible'

So I left my friend in his positive mood, convinced that he was soon to become an MP, and walked to my bank. They already knew me, so there was no problem in withdrawing £100, which I reckoned would cover the deposit on the farm and much more. Then I hurried to Lime Street and took a train to Manchester. Time was getting on and I wanted to get to the agents before they closed.

I had a compartment to myself and as I looked out of the window at the bleak landscape of Chat Moss, I thought about the farm and how it could be made successful; a small flock of sheep, a couple of cows for milk, butter and cheese, some chickens for my sister to look after, and to teach my daughter to raise. They might also have a couple of goats, because they are easy to feed and their meat is very tasty. And one of the less stoney fields could be planted with a crop to feed the animals.

At last we were into the industrial mass of Manchester. When I got to the station, I checked the trains to Shrewsbury, and discovered that there was one quite late, so if I changed my mind and decided to go to meet Nan it would be fine.

I reached the Land Agents just as they were about to close, but the thought of making some money out of a derelict piece of land, made them welcoming, though surprisingly unenthusiastic about the farm itself.

'You do know that it's in the middle of know-where.'

'Indeed. It was my home for more than twenty years.'

'Aah! And you do know that it has been sadly neglected'

'Yes, I was there yesterday.

Oh!

'I have spent many years in America, and have seen some men make a great deal out of nothing. I intend to do the same.'

'I thought there was something unusual about the way you spoke.'

'Yes, though I still see myself as Welsh.

'But a man who has seen something of the world'

'Indeed.' I didn't tell them that the world I had seen had included a dreadful view from a prison in the midst of this very city.

By the time the business was signed and sealed it was very late and I was hungry, so I left the agents and made my way to a fine restaurant and congratulated myself on becoming the owner of a small farm in the middle of North Wales.

Full of fine food and a glass of good wine- a taste I had learned from my father-in-law in New York- I started to walk back to the station intending to catch a train back to Liverpool. It was nearly midnight and on the nearest platform stood a train about to leave for the West of England, stopping at Crewe, Shrewsbury and several stations beyond. I suddenly made up my mind to board that train and get to Shrewsbury as soon as possible. Then I would go to the hospital, see the matron, offer a donation to hospital funds and insist that she let me see Nan straight away

The journey began comfortably enough. My carriage was well back from the engine, so I hardly heard the sound of the locomotive. The compartment was clean and warm. There were three fellow travellers; opposite me sat an ancient clergyman, in faded grey clothes, reading a serous-looking book, silently but with lips moving as he read. On my side sat a young couple, very close to one another, as if newly married or at least in deeply in love. I didn't interrupt them with idle chatter, but settled my head against the headboard and tried to snooze. Soon I was actually asleep, and it wasn't till I heard someone shouting, 'Crewe Station. All change for Birmingham and London'- that I came to and remembered where I was. The young couple left and an older man took their place. He was well dressed and obviously well fed. As he went to sit down there was clang, the carriage jerked and he sat down abruptly.

'Ah, that's the rest of the train, some carriages from Glasgow and a mail carriage. We're going to be a long load for the engine to pull the rest of the way.'

I detected a brummy note in his accent. He took some important looking documents out of a briefcase and began to read, as the train jerked again and the engine noise increased as it began to pull its heavy load.

We made our way through Cheshire and North Shropshire at a steady pace, I knew the route fairly well, from recent visits. When we passed through the little station at Wem, I realised we were almost at Shrewsbury and I began to think about seeing my daughter after all these years.

When we finally began the last descent into Shrewsbury I began to suspect that something was wrong. Instead of decreasing speed as I knew we should to get round the steep curve just before Shrewsbury Station we were going faster and faster. I glanced at my fellow passengers to see if they shared my worry, but the clergy man was engrossed in his book and the man beside me was making notes in pencil against the print in his documents,

The train began to sway with our increased speed and the wheels of our carriage squealed against the rails. I became very concerned and stood up in the compartment, saying, 'Something's wrong. We should be slowing down.'

Suddenly there was a tremendous bang, the compartment shook, then rose upward. My head collided with the roof and I saw no more.

Chapter Twenty Two

Nan woke to the loud clanging of a bell. At first she thought it must be in her dreams, but what would a loud bell be doing in a dream set in the Vyrnwy Valley, where she was walking with a man she could not really see: a shadowy form but warm towards her.

The other students in the room began to stir as the bell continued its deafening clangour. Then a woman walked into the room and began to shout above the sound of the bell.

'You must all get up at once and dress in your warmest, most waterproof clothes and come down to the main entrance. Please be no longer than 15 minutes. I want you all there by 2.30. Now hurry!'

All the girls were now awake but totally confused.

'What on earth is going on?'

'It must be a fire drill.'

'In the middle of the night?

'Perhaps it's a real fire?

'But that's not the quickest way out of the building.'

Sometimes these speeches were broken off while clothes were dragged over heads.

At last all were ready and went down quickly to the entrance. where they were formed into pairs, each student accompanied by a more experience nurse. While this was being organised a burly man in a large red coat spoke, very loudly.

'Now listen very carefully. There has been a rail accident just outside the station. There will be many injured. You will see sights you aint seen before. So if anyone aint up to it drop out now.'

Nan wasn't sure she was up to it, but the nurse beside her smiled and whispered, 'You'll be fine with me'

The man spoke again. 'Right, follow me. Quick March!'

Perhaps he had been a soldier, thought Nan, as they left the building and marched down Castle Hill. At the bottom they turned into the station and climbed the steps up to the platform. Then to the surprise of most they stepped down from the platform onto the rails. Here each pair was issued with a lamp, so that they would not trip over debris from the crash. In the distance they could hear the moans and cries of the injured and soon they came to the first signs of the crash. The huge locomotive was slewed across the rails, on its side, steam still oozing from its innards.

'Reminds me of a dead elephant I saw in India'

Nan knew that Amanda had spent her childhood in India where her father was an officer in the army. Nan had never seen an elephant at all.

A carriage had come to rest above the locomotive, and one of the pairs was sent to find any injured passengers. Nan wondered how anyone in that smashed carriage, which had crashed into the locomotive with such force, could possibly still be still alive.

'I'm Nurse Probert by the way. You are?'

'Nan Morris. Student Nurse.'

Nan and her partner walked on and met other rescuers carrying stretchers back towards the station. Some rescuers had arrived even before news got to the hospital.

'Brave souls,' said Nurse Probert.

The state of the carriages was dreadful. Some were piled one on top the next. Others had been pushed sideways and turned on their sides.

The man in the red coat approached Nan's partner, saying' This is yours. It's not too badly broken. Go through that gap at the end and work your way along the corridor. Shout for help if you need it.'

Just then another stretcher went by and Nan saw a man- guessing by his trousers- with his head entirely hidden in bandages, being rushed as fast as his bearers could carry him towards help on the station.

Nan looked at the carriage beside her. The wheels were almost as tall as herself. How could she get aboard? But the man in the red coat came closer and picked her up as if she was weightless and deposited her in the carriage. Then Nurse Probert handed her a bag and waited for the man to lift her up. She was a bit heavier but soon she was up beside Nan, who asked as she handed back the bag, 'What's in here?'

'Medical supplies,' she said, 'Right, let's get on.'

It was very dark in the carriage, but they found their way into the first compartment. It was empty, or so they thought, until they looked up and saw a woman lying in the luggage rack, where she had been thrown by the impact of the crash. Blood was pouring from her head. She muttered a weak, 'Help, help me.' Somehow, they managed to get her down from the rack and lay her on the seat. Then Nan held her head while the nurse bandaged it securely. Then Probert gave the woman an injection and soon she was asleep.

'A spot of morphine. Now she will sleep while we move on.'

In the next carriage was a young man lying on the floor. He was obviously in pain and when they saw the angle of his lower leg they realised why. The bone was broken and the upper part was showing through his trouser leg. This was something they could not deal without further equipment, so Nurse Probert gave him a shot of morphine and told Nan to leave the carriage and find some stretcher bearers. Nan climbed down out of the carriage, with considerable difficulty and almost no modestry, and called for stretcher bearers. She was in luck as two men approached and asked what she required. The men climbed up into the carriage and soon returned with the young man on the stretcher, moaning at each awkward movement as he was lifted out of the carriage and taken towards the station, with Probert at his side in case he needed comfort.

Nan managed to scramble back into the carriage and went along to the last compartment. She was met by a strange sight; an elderly clergyman sat unharmed, slumped in his seat with a book on his lap and his eyes open. But when Nan looked closely, she realised he was not breathing and when she checked he had no pulse. The shock of the crash must have killed him but as this rear end of the carriage was not thrown about so violently, he remained in his seat. She went to the window which had lost its glass and shouted to a passing man that there was a dead body in the compartment. Then she noticed that the sill was covered in blood and large segments of glass had fallen to the ground. If anyone had been sitting here, they would have suffered bad cuts, and probably been thrown out of the window. Then she remembered the man on the stretcher with his head covered in bandages.

Nan waited until some men came to take the corpse away. When they had gone, she glanced round the compartment and saw a fine overcoat neatly folded on the rack. She took it down and examined it, in case the owners name should be inside. When she saw that there was indeed a name embroidered on the inside pocket she practically dropped the coat with shock.

In stitches the name said, 'Mr H. Morris' She burst into tears, then carrying the coat she hurried back to the station.

As Nan made her way back to the hospital her head was filled with dreadful images: that dead clergyman with his open eyes staring blindly at a book; the young man's broken leg with a bone protruding through his trouser leg; the woman's head wound pouring blood. She felt proud that she had faced them all, but the sight that disturbed her most was the man on the stretcher with his head entirely bound in bandages. Was he the one who had fallen through the window of that last compartment and left his coat on the rack. Was he in fact the Huw Morris who was coming to meet her? Was that badly injured man her father? She must get to the hospital soon and check the wards for that man.

Nan was exhausted as she reached the entrance to the hospital, after the long walk back to the station and the climb up Castle Hill. Unfortunately, she was met at the entrance by a ward sister, called Crumpton, who did not like her because she was young and pretty whereas Crumpton herself was middle aged and very plain.

'Well Morris. What brings you back so soon. Got tired of seeing a few injuries have you.'

Nan was about to reply angrily when she heard a familiar voice. It was Nurse Probert,' Ah, Miss Morris, good to see you back. I've been hearing good things about you. Time now for a rest and something to eat. The refectory has been opened especially.'

Nan suddenly felt her stomach crying out for something to eat, but she wanted to find the owner of that coat.

'I found this coat in the last compartment. I should go up to the ward and find out who it belongs to.'

'Give it to me, Morris. Only surgical staff are allowed up there.'

Crumpton took hold of the coat. Nan objected. She wanted to know if her father was among the injured.

'But!'

'It's all right,' said Probert. 'Sister Crumpton will make sure it gets to the right patient.

'Fine coat this' said Crumpton and Nan was not so sure it would get back to Huw.' But she could not refuse to hand it over.

Probert said, 'Now, off you go and get something to eat, then have a rest before your duties start, and, well done Morris.'

Nan looked at the coat under Crumpton's arm. Then accepted defeat and went down to the refectory

After a very quick breakfast Nan remained in the refectory. She would have liked to talk to some of her fellow students but at that time none had appeared.

Her hunger assuaged, she no longer felt tired, and had no wish to return to her room. She felt restless. Crumpton had stopped her going to look for her father, and she no longer had that coat to use as an excuse for visiting the ward.

The refectory was in the basement and Nan knew that steps had been built up to the street as an emergency exit, so she would be able to avoid Crumpton at the main entrance. A short walk around the town would help her to forget the dreadful scenes of that rail crash and to lessen her own frustration.

The town seemed to be awake early that morning. Probably news of the crash had spread quickly and people were eager to see for themselves. Nan had no wish to go near the station so she walked in the opposite direction and soon came to the Market Square. It was almost light by now and she watched the stalls being prepared for the market.

There was a woman standing under the market hall who did not look like a stallholder at all. She was dressed in a sober tweed suit and her hair was pulled back tightly and fixed into a bun, so that she looked very severe. Nan wondered what she was doing in the square but she hadn't got the courage to ask her. Nan realised it wasn't her business and walked on towards St Chad's Church and into the Quarry Park.

Soon she came to the place where the Circus tent had stood. There was no sign of it now. But the vision of that man with wandering hands-what was his name? Norman? Yes. One of many men she felt angry about at the moment. There was also Mr Noble, who had turned her mother away, when she most needed help, and who had never shown herself the slightest iota of affection. Indeed, if it hadn't been for Ella's constant love and care, she would have left home much sooner. Then there was her own father, though she longed to see him now, but what use had he been all those years ago. He had made her mother pregnant, then disappeared, and he had done nothing to find his daughter until very recently. No, thought Nan, I don't have much faith in the male sex.

She walked by the river, then into the Dingle, where she sat in the strengthening sun for a while. Her weariness returned and her eyes began to close. A duck and drake came quacking loudly across the little lake in the hope of some food and she decided it was time to move on.

When she reached the Market Square, she heard a rowdy group in one corner jeering at someone in their midst. Nan realised it was the woman she had seen under the Market Hall.

Now the woman was standing on a wooden box addressing the crowd. She was obviously upset by the crowd's response; her face was red and some of her hair had slipped out of the pins and hung down over her cheeks.

'All I want is votes for women.'

The men in the crowd were heckling and her voice was too quiet to be heard above them.

'What you need is a good man to rough you up a bit. Give you a good doing. Know what I mean' This was said in a screechy voice by a little man standing right in front of her.'

A voice from the back spoke.' I wouldn't touch her with a barge pole. She's an ugly witch.'

And so it went on. The men made fun of her looks and laughed at her ideas. The few women in the crowd gave her no support, afraid of the men beside them. Nan became more and more angry. Her mind was in a turmoil. She walked away from the crowd and towards the council offices. She picked up a loose cobble, and flung it towards the big windows, shouting, 'Votes for women'.

Years of playing cricket with the boys in the village had given her a strong arm and an accurate throw. There was loud smash and the pane shattered. Nan burst into tears. Unfortunately, a policeman was standing close by, keeping the peace. He immediately apprehended Nan and gripping her with his large, strong arm led her away to the police station.

Chapter 23

Huw woke to a white world. He could see nothing but a universe of white light. Was he in heaven? But surely there was no pain in heaven. And there was certainly pain here, wherever it was. There was a stinging pain in his head, his face, his hands; a throbbing, sharp pain. He wanted to howl with the pain, but when he tried it came out as a muffled murmur. Then there came a voice, from somewhere in the white universe. An angel perhaps.

'How are you, Sir? Are you in pain?'

It was a woman's voice. Huw was surprised to find that although he could not speak, he could nod his head, but that increased the pain. He gave a slight moan.

The voice came again, 'Well, I can do something about that.'

The woman's voice came closer as she moved something from the lower part of his face. Then she put something in his mouth and put a cup of water to his lips. He involuntarily swallowed whatever she had put in his mouth. Almost immediately the pain eased, then he slipped easily back into sleep.

Huw remembered little of the accident. Yes, he remembered the train going faster and faster, when it should have been slowing down. He remembered getting up to look out of the window, to try find out what was happening. Then the carriage suddenly slewed across the rails, flinging him through the window, which shattered into fragments, catching his head and hands as he fell. Then nothing. Till now, when he opened his eyes on this white world.

When he woke next time there was a man's voice, and hands very carefully removing something from his head. Then suddenly he could see. He was in a bed, in a hospital, a white coated man was studying his scalp.

'Are you able to give us your name?

'I am Morris. Huw Morris.'

'Well Mr Huw Morris- I am Doctor Newberry by the way- and

you're a very lucky man. You have some nasty and, I suspect, painful cuts on your face and head, and some on your hands as well'

Huw looked at his hands which were tightly bandaged.

'But amazingly the glass did not penetrate your eyes, and only slightly cut one of your ears, and thank goodness, opened no veins in your neck and only some cuts in your skull, where we were able to remove the glass and bandage you up. The pain will lessen, and you will heal quite quickly.'

The nurse who had accompanied the doctor suddenly spoke.

'What a remarkable coincidence. I have been working this morning with a student nurse called Morris. And a very brave young woman she was. Oh, and I have your coat, or rather I know where it is.'

'I don't care so much about the coat. But have you really been working with my daughter? I only just learned that she was here in the hospital. I was coming to meet her when the accident happened

It would have been our first meeting. I know that will sound strange, but it is true.

'Doctor, should I go and fetch the coat, and enquire about Miss Morris. I believe she is called Nan.'

Huw nodded, less painfully this time.

'She will probably be resting in the student room.'

'Yes, I think a meeting of father and daughter would do well for my patient. What do you think, Mr Morris?

'I feel better already.'

'Then go ahead, Nurse Probert. Meanwhile I will make the patient more presentable.'

Nurse Probert hurried away. The doctor checked the scalp and applied some appointment, then rebandaged Huw's head, this time leaving the eyes uncovered.

When the nurse returned it was with a look of consternation.

The doctor asked, 'What is it nurse?'

'She cannot be found. She left the hospital for a walk into town and has not been seen since. Two orderlies have been sent to look for her. It is very strange.'

'It is indeed,' said Huw. 'Trains crash, Daughter goes missing. It is as if we were never destined to meet.'

Chapter 24

The mystery deepened. Nan did not return from her walk, even at evening meal time. More staff were sent out to look for her, but without success. When darkness fell the police were informed. The policeman who had arrested Nan had gone on leave for a week and had not bothered to inform anyone else.

I became increasingly concerned over the next few days. I had read about young women being abducted, but did such things happen in a small market town like Shrewsbury. I was healing fast, but it was frustrating to be kept in a hospital bed when I should be out looking for my daughter. Doctor Newberry had informed me that I should be well enough to be discharged by Friday. Meanwhile I longed to be up and out and sometimes considered discharging myself. But then the pain would return and I knew I was not ready yet.

On Thursday I received excellent news; Phillip had been elected as a Member of Parliament. With the help of Doctor Newberry I sent a telegram congratulating him, but I would soon discover how important my friendship with a Member of Parliament would turn out to be.

Where on earth had Nan gone? Surely, she would not have left Shrewsbury, when she knew that her father was coming to meet her. Had she gone back to her home of many years with John Noble and Ella? Surely not, especially when she had just left on such bad terms with John. After all, she knew now that he had turned her mother out of his home when she most needed his support and eventually, she had died because of his action.

When Friday came, I knew I had to get out of hospital and find my daughter. I informed Doctor Newberry, who gave me a check-over and declared.

'You'll be fine, if you don't over exert yourself. Keep your hat on and wear gloves until the cuts are thoroughly healed. And wash regularly. Now go and find that daughter of yours, where-ever she is. You will need to pay for your care here of course, but from what I hear that will not be a problem.'

I paid for my hospital care and left midday on Friday. My first action on leaving the hospital was to purchase a local newspaper, in case there was some clue as to Nan's disappearance.

I sat on a bench at the top of Pride Hill and flicked through the newspaper. I was about to crumple the newspaper and throw it in the bin, when I noticed a brief report in the police section.

Young woman arrested for criminal damage.

Miss Nan Morris, aged 18, was arrested in the Market Square, last Tuesday for throwing a loose cobble stone and breaking a window in the Council Offices. When apprehended she simply said, 'Votes for women. Bloody men'

She will appear before the Magistrates on Monday morning.

At first all I could do was chuckle at her words. Then I thought. 'The poor girl will be terrified. I have to find her. The police station? As soon as I thought of this possibility, I asked a passer-by, the whereabouts of the police station and was directed to Swan Hill on the other side of the Market Square.

The building was old and dark. Inside was a desk with a tall thin police officer behind it. He looked down from a height and asked,' Can I help?'

'Yes, a young woman was possibly brought here. Under arrest for breaking a window in the Market Square. Her name was Nan Morris. I am her father and I would like to see her.'

'Well, she baint 'ere. Sounds like she be on remand up at Shoosbry Jail.'

'In Jail! Surely not. She's no criminal.'

'Ah well. She'll be up before the magistrates on Monday.'

'Will it be possible to visit her?'

'You'll have to ask at the prison.'

I made my way across the town towards Shrewsbury Gaol. I knew that this was one of the more humane places of incarceration, following the Howard reforms, but I was still horrified by the thought of my daughter in there among the dross of society, but then I remembered I had once been a prison inmate too. My treatment in that prison had been rough by the officers and the prisoners alike.

As I crossed the wooden footbridge over the station, I could see tall cranes working to remove the debris from the railway lines so that normal service could return. When I left the foot-bridge I turned right and was soon near the prison entrance, with its statue of John Howard, the prison reformer, set into the brick wall above the door.

I rang a bell and was informed by a voice from within that it was too late for me to be admitted, If I wanted admittance I must write to the Governor, explaining my reasons and await his reply. I put on my bossiest voice and informed the person inside that my friend, who was a Member of Parliament, was coming to examine the prison in the near future and would not be pleased to hear how I had been treated.

The door suddenly opened with an apology from the prison officer who had opened it. I was taken to see a more senior member of the prison staff, where I explained that I had reason to interview a young woman called Nan Morris, to ask how she had been treated since she had entered the prison.

When Nan came into the room, she looked very small and pale. She was obviously frightened by the prison officer who accompanied her. Luckily, she did not immediately recognise me as her father, so I explained that I was making a report about recent admissions to the prison and I had been given her name.

'So how have you been treated?'

'Well enough'

'Do you have any complaints?

'The cell is filthy and these clothes are very rough.'

The prison officer was not pleased about these complaints.

'Them as go throwing stones at important winders gets put in gaol. After all You might have missed and hit someone instead.'

'My aim is very good. And it was in an important cause.'

The prisoner officer laughed, 'What, Votes for women. Never!'

I looked Nan in the face and spoke seriously. 'You realise that you will face the magistrates on Monday. You must try for their mercy'

The prison officer could not see her smile as she asked.

'What's that to you, sir?

'I have to attend to see that you are treated fairly.'

'How, Sir, should I behave in front of these important people?'

'You should be modest and remorseful.'

'I will try my best sir.'

Another smile, showing no remorse at all.

'Time to go.' said the officer, as he turned to the door.

Nan meanwhile approached me and whispered. 'Thank you for your advice' then very quietly she added, 'Father.'

On Monday morning I made my way to the Magistrates Court, where I was informed that Nan's case would be third. I sat near the back of the court and looked around. It was a handsome building, appropriate for its serious purpose. Soon we were asked to stand and the magistrates appeared. First came a small wizened old man, who had probably been a magistrate for a hundred years. He was followed by mountain of a man, who looked as if he might be a butcher, with a very florid face and a low gruff voice. Then last came a man who could have been a woman. He was neatly dressed and his longish fair hair was well cut. But, of course, all magistrates must be male.

At my own trial, in crown court, it was all bewigged judges

and lawyers and a row of angry looking jurymen. I had been terrified from the start and knew what the result would be. I hoped for Nan's sake that these more ordinary men had more humanity in their hearts.

The first case was a young man caught poaching on one of the large estates surrounding Shrewsbury. A few years ago, this would have got him hanged or transported, but things had improved slightly so he was only sentenced to a year in jail. He was still upset because he had a young family and did not know how they would manage without him, and it was because they had been very hungry that he had taken a rabbit and a pheasant: the rabbit to eat and the pheasant to sell. I thought of Jed and how hungry we would have been without his ability with a gun

I longed to shout out in his defence but he was unrepresented and was led off swearing at the world.

The next case was of a young girl, about Nan's age, accused of prostitution. She explained in clear language that her step-father had raped her, then turned her out onto the streets, where her only way of making a living was to offer her body for money. There were signs of shock and horror on the faces of magistrates one and two but the third bent his head towards them and whispered for some time. Then the large one, who seemed to be in charge said gruffly, 'Very well' He cleared his throat and said,

'We are saddened to hear of your plight, but in no way can we condone your behaviour.' He paused. I thought if I could meet that step-father I should enjoy giving him the hiding of his life.

'Mr Bradbury has informed me that Lady Cockshut is prepared to offer you a place at her establishment as a house maid, on the understanding that your behaviour is perfect. Do you accept that chance?

The girl smiled and answered, 'That's wonderful. Of course I accept.

'Very well. You will be taken to her home immediately. But you must agree to pay a fine of £20 to the court, in instalments from your weekly wage. Case dismissed.'

I was pleased to hear the outcome, but imagined that £20 would take a very long time to repay on a maid's wages.

There was a pause in proceedings. Then Nan appeared in the witness box. Her head was lowered modestly and her voice was soft and submissive as she took the oath.

The case was described in slightly mocking terms. The magistrates had already decided that as it was a first offence and the accused was a well-mannered young woman, that she would be given a caution and pay a £10 fine. Nan was informed that her father was prepared to pay her fine, then asked if she had anything to say. Sensibly she simply apologised for her stupidity and informed the magistrates that it would never happen again.

I had to wait at the cashier's counter while the paperwork came through, then I paid the fine and made my way to the door where those who had been released came out. Shortly Nan arrived, looking rather less modest and we faced one another for a while. So this was my daughter, the result of my love for Amy and hers for me. Her looks were mine rather than her mothers, but she shone with youth and health. While I was studying her, she was studying me.

Then she spoke in a soft Shropshire burr 'Thank you father, for paying my fine.'

'Well I am your father, even though I was not aware of your existence until a few weeks ago.'

'Why were you not able to help mother when she needed it all those years ago? '

Because I was in prison, wrongfully accused of something I did not do.'

'And what of all the years since?'

'Oh, that's a very long story. And now we've met I have plenty of time to tell it. Meanwhile let us enjoy one another's company'

Then I clasped her to me, saying, 'Nan. Oh Nan.' and tears filled both our eyes.

Chapter 25

I booked a room for Nan at my hotel that evening. She had explained to me that she must return to the hospital in the morning to continue her studies. I told her that there was no need as she would be coming to live with me at Ty Craig. She replied that she would like that but not until she had become a nurse. I found that she was an honest and straight-forward girl. She was astonished that I had so much money: paying fines and booking hotel rooms without a thought. I told her briefly about my gold prospecting days. Her eyes opened wide and she exclaimed, 'That sounds so exciting.'

'It was,' I said. 'but I also lost a very good friend in the Klondyke. The cold was intense and he was already ill'

'By the way' she said. 'What shall I call you? Would you prefer 'father' or your name?

I thought for a moment, then said, 'I don't feel that I have been a proper father, so perhaps you should simply call me Huw.'

'Very well, you shall be 'Huw'.

We both went to bed early that night, after our eventful day. In the morning we shared breakfast in the dining room, then made our way to the hospital. The matron invited Nan into her office, but I must stay outside. When Nan returned she was in tears.

I made her sit beside me in the tiled hallway and asked, 'What is it Nan? What's wrong?'

'They refuse to take me back. No one with a criminal record can be a nurse.'

'That's ridiculous. You only broke a window. And in a good cause.'

'It wasn't so much Matron, but she had this sister with her called Crumpton. She hates me. She had influenced the Matron, I am sure. What do I do now?'

'You come with me to Ty Craig.

'My mother told me of it. She liked it very much.'

'That is where I lived as a child and young man, with my mother until she died, my father and my dear sister, after whom you are surely named.'

'My mother spoke often of your sister, Nan. I cannot remember much because I was very young, but there was something about her not being able to talk.'

'Yes, Nan had a problem with her speech, but she could make herself understood.'

'So where is this sister of yours'

I'm not entirely sure. When my father died, she had to leave the farm. I believe she went to live with a cousin in South Wales.'

'Then we must find her. And if we are going back to Ty Graig then she must come too.'

I consulted my Bradshaw's Railway Guide and discovered that we must take the train to Cardiff and change to another line that would take us to Merthyr Tydfil. Nan sadly returned to the hospital to collect her few belongings and met me at the station where I had purchased our tickets, having discovered that the route south of Shrewsbury was working again. When we met, Nan asked immediately,

'Why Huw, what is wrong? You are so pale.'

'It's...'

'Oh of course, I understand. You are worried that the train will crash. But that was a tragic accident. The railways generally are very safe.'

'Dear Nan, you are quite right. And here we are, look, a splendid locomotive, come to take us safely in our fine carriage all the way to Cardiff.'

But it was not until many miles on our journey, having passed through Ludlow, that the sweat left my brow and I began to relax and enjoy sitting beside my pretty daughter as we shared the fine landscape beyond the window. I was also surprised that she seemed so little affected by her own involvement in that disastrous event.

'The fact is, Huw -I know that we agreed that I should call you that.' I nodded in agreement. 'On that dreadful night I was too busy doing what we had to do, to notice the horror of it. Now it just seems like a terrible nightmare, and I am glad to be awake again. Thank goodness you have recovered from your injuries and we can be together, father and daughter. She gave my arm a little squeeze. I smiled and returned that squeeze, and felt the life pulsing through her slim young arm.

Our travelling companions all left the train at Hereford.

Nan suddenly asked,' 'Tell me more about your time in America'

I started at the beginning with my first time in New York and tried to keep the story going chronologically. There were just two events I omitted; the woman I abandoned in Green River Valley and the wife who died in childbirth during my second time in New York. I didn't want to feel guilty again about the first and I knew that the second would have my eyes filling with tears.

When we reached Cardiff, I was astonished at what a large place it had become. I had read that the King Edward V11 had made it a city two years before. It had become prosperous because of its port, from which Welsh coal was exported to the world. From the train as it drew into Cardiff Central Station we could see some very fine buildings, but there was no time to get out and explore. We must get on to Merthyr Tydfil and find my sister.

When I saw the train on which we were to continue our journey my nervousness returned. The locomotive was a scruffy little tank engine which did not look capable of hauling the six dilapidated carriages attached to it. I insisted we took the last carriage, as I thought it looked the most substantial.

Our journey through the suburbs of Cardiff began smoothly enough, despite the banging and clanking of our carriage wheels on the rails. The line here was quite flat so we made reasonable speed. Nan sat close and tried to stop me worrying. In the distance I saw the coal mines that had given the area its prosperity and after a while the land began to rise into misty hills, so the train slowed and the locomotive made more noise with the effort of pulling us up an increasing incline. After an hour or so we were approaching our destination, and what a gloomy place it seemed to be.

Merthyr Tydfil was a much larger town than I had expected. The streets of mainly terraced houses climbed steeply into the mountains, which were black with rain. We donned our raincoats, left the train and began to climb towards the centre of the town. We passed many an industrial premises that was empty, even partly demolished, and even more that announced 'For Sale'.

By the time we reached what appeared to be the town centre we were exhausted and looked about for somewhere to sit and rest. We discovered a small open space with some stubby grass and a couple of untrimmed trees, and beneath them a bench where we could sit for a while and think what to do. The bench was already occupied by an old man, but he was happy to move along and let us sit beside him.

The old man asked, in that peculiarly South Wales way of speaking. 'I've not seen you around here before.'

I answered,' No, it's our first visit to Merthyr Tydfil'

'Ah, it's from North Wales you are. I can hear it in your voice. And who's this pretty young woman beside you?

'That's my daughter, Nan.'

'Well, welcome you are to my town, but a sad place it is nowadays.'

'It does seem rather depressed.'

That's the very word, depressed. Everything's gone or going, but half a century ago, when I was a young man, this was the largest town in Wales. Iron works everywhere, coal mines, quarries. Jobs galore. All nearly gone. No work. Just poverty now.

'How sad,' said Nan.

'So what are you doing here, in Merthyr?

'We've come to find my sister. She is also called Nan.'

'Oh, don't you know where she lives?'

'I lost touch with her for many years. I was abroad.'

'Such a pity. What is she like?'

'Well the most noticeable thing, is she has difficulty speaking.

'Oh, you mean the woman that does for the Dr Morris who lives in that posh house off Grove Lane.'

Nan gasped and smiled. My eyebrows raised in shock as I said 'Yes, I am her brother, Huw.'

The man smiled widely 'I can tell you exactly where she lives'

'That's wonderful,' I said.

'Well you see, I take a walk every morning, along the same streets, and everyday I see her walking the same streets, so I say "Good morning" and she replies in her own kind of way.'

'Does she look well?'

'Quite well, for a servant.'

'But she's not a servant. She lives with her cousin.'

'Cousin or not, she is treated as a servant. Cleans the steps, fetches the shopping in two heavy baskets. Takes the children to school and brings them home. She always has smile for me, but I know she is not happy.'

'What is this doctor Morris like?'

'Not a likeable man. Thinks he's above everyone else. And charges far more for his services than any other doctor in town. I'd rather die than go to him.'

'Oh dear. Well at least you can show us where he lives.'

'Of course. I'll walk part of the way with you.'

So we set off, up the steep streets, past the Town Hall, the post office and a small hotel, then into a better part of the town, with larger, better built houses having gardens at the front and rear, but the roads became steeper until our guide suddenly stopped and gasped.

'Oh, that's enough for me. I'm getting on you know. But if you go up there, it's the last house on the left, very grand.'

We said our goodbyes with much thanks from me. Nan remarked how incredible it was that the one person in the town we had spoken to, should be able to help us. That made us both feel much better about Merthyr Tydfil.

Nan and I were able to walk faster now, she being young and me reasonably fit. Soon the house came into view, a striking place with a pillared portico, turrets at the corners, and a garden full of tall pines and weeping willows. We climbed the many steps and read the polished brass which announced James Morris, followed by the several letters of his medical qualifications. I rang the equally polished bell. There was pause, then the door opened and a middle-aged woman stood staring at me.

'Oh Nan, Nan.'

Of course, she was at least seventeen years older than when I had last seen her, but her tired, lined face was a shock. And all the fun had gone out of her flashing, dark eyes. I hugged her tight, and after a few seconds she hugged me back.

'Is it really you, Huw? Then who is this?'

'This is Amy's child. She is called Nan, after you.'

The tears flowed from my sister's eyes as she hugged Nan.

My sister led us into the hallway. The floor was intricately tiled and a grand staircase led up to the bedrooms.

Nan could not take her eyes off me. She asked me to tell her where I had been all these years, but before I could begin, a large man with florid features and a bushy beard came out from a room at the side. He stopped in astonishment.

'Who are you? What are you doing in my house?

'I am your cousin Huw. I have come to see my sister.'

'Oh, the jailbird of the family'

'That was a long time ago. And I was unjustly imprisoned.'

'They all say that.'

'And who is this young woman? Your mistress I suppose.'

I was about to punch this unpleasant man, but my daughter spoke up.

'How dare you. Huw is my father.'

The man smirked and said, 'Well Huw. Why are you here?'

'I've already said, I have come to collect my sister and take her home.'

'But you can't do that. We have guests this evening. Nan must cook.'

'You obviously don't understand. Nan is not your servant, though it is quite obvious you have treated her as such. She came to you for help and support.'

'And is very grateful. She was turned out of her home in North Wales.'

'But I now own that farm and she is coming back to it.'

'How can you afford a farm?'

'Because I am a rich man. Much richer than you.' I turned to Nan. 'Go and pack your bags, dear sister, we have a train to catch.

Doctor Morris spluttered. 'This is outrageous. All these years we have supported her'

I took out my wallet. 'How much do I owe you?'

Doctor Morris stood flabbergasted as I flicked through a wad of banknotes.

My sister hurried upstairs to pack. I handed Morris several notes. He took and pocketed them, but still seemed in a dream. My sister returned.

I thanked the doctor for his hospitality. Young Nan giggled at this irony. My sister couldn't get out of that house fast enough and soon we were walking down the streets of Merthyr Tydfil towards the station, father, sister and daughter arm in arm.

Chapter 26

At four o-clock John Noble dismissed his class and watched them leave the school. Some of the oldest boys, soon to be released into the world of work, grabbed a pig's bladder and passed it from one to another as they hurtled down the lane. A few of the more mature lads were more interested in walking with the prettiest girls and chatting to them. Most of the girls had younger brothers and sisters to collect from the infant's class. John's latest young assistant was a quiet calm girl who looked after her charges well and taught them efficiently. She would easily pass her examinations and move on to be a qualified teacher in a couple of years.

Soon there was only one girl left from his own class, poor Maria, who dreaded going home, to a father who beat her mother and herself, out of frustration because he was jobless and liked the bottle too much. John knew that little Maria had a crush on him, and treated her with neutral courtesy. Finally, even Maria forced herself to leave

Once the children had gone, John hurried to the school house and changed his clothes. Returning to the kitchen, he picked up a piece of an apple pie that Ella had made that afternoon, swallowed it with obvious enjoyment, but did not thank his wife, or make any comment. They rarely spoke these days. The rift in their marriage had begun long ago, when he had told Amy to leave home because she was with child. It widened further when she died. Then, with Nan leaving as well, things had got much worse. Ella had enjoyed her granddaughter's company, whereas John resented her, as a constant reminder of her mother's relationship with that hated Welshman and her unnecessary death.

John set off through the village, as far as the entrance to Moreton Hall. His friendship with the Squire, Robert Moreton, who lived at the Hall had long since faded, partly because they moved in such different circles now, but also because Ella seemed more alive in Squire Moreton's company, than she ever was with John.

The headteacher was glad there was no-one about, especially any of his pupils or their parents. He was far too occupied with his own thoughts, which these days tended to be gloomy.

How much longer would he have to continue as head teacher? The school ran itself, the attendance was good, the behaviour excellent; he could not remember the last time he had to resort to the cane. But it was all so boring. John was now almost in his sixties. He still had to attend the church so that he maintained his position as head of a church school and the constant repetition of the old prayers and hymns gave him some peace. It wasn't exactly belief but a comfort to his troubled mind.

Ella refused to accompany him. She had been a firm believer, but the death of her daughter had caused a change, now she would not even go into the church yard.

But it was the curriculum that John despised the most. There had been little change since John became a teacher thirty years ago. Religious teaching was a good deal more interesting given by the latest young Vicar who one by one had replaced the evil Whiting, but it was all mere storytelling, except for the boring catechism and such like. Geography still mostly showed the Empire, in all the pink parts of the globe. History promoted the latest monarch and his forbears, even though he was a glutton and a womaniser. Arithmetic prepared his pupils for the daily use of numbers in sums of money they would never have. Science did not exist.

John felt that his years as a teacher must end soon. But he had to provide for Ella however distant they had become. And what else could he do. His life as a missionary had been a failure. He had no money to take up farming. He was not a fit man, despite his daily walk. He knew he had put on weight and even a short walk tired him and caused breathlessness. He had no real health problems, just a vague feeling of malaise.

That had to change. He must do more exercise. He would start now. He would take the path beside the wood and walk to the top of the hill, as he used to do at one time, and enjoy the view over the valley. Yes, he must start using his body more and become a fit man again.

He took the path which ran beside the wood beyond which lay Moreton Hall, and where John had once sought shelter from men carrying guns and seeking poachers. By the time he reached the start of the Long Hill he was exhausted, his heart was thumping in his chest and he gasped for breath. But when he sat on a tree stump and looked down it was all worthwhile. He had not seen this view for many years.

Some of the fields he saw below him had belonged to his father and was where he had lived as a child. He remembered his mother cleaning his knee when he had fallen whilst running with his favourite dog, and his father explaining about some aspect of farming. Unfortunately, John had no interest in that, so they remained at odds. Then he spotted the field where that Welsh woman had initiated him into sex. Now sex had become a problem between Ella and himself. She had lost interest and he practically had to force her. Even then it was not always successful as his own powers were waning and his erection often failed.

When they first met Ella was a lovely young woman and John was a virile male so sex was frequent and enjoyable. Soon Ella was pregnant with young John. Ella could not accept John's unreasonable behaviour towards Amy, and longed for her to return.

Next John recognised that fateful field where a young woman's body had been found, murdered and decaying, as the last field of barley was harvested. He particularly remembered the hair covered in blood and her skin showing bites where hungry animals had nibbled. The police had soon ceased to seek the murderer, but John went on with his investigations until the murderer was caught and the Reverend Whiting, curse his name, was hanged in Shrewsbury Gaol.

Ironically, that young woman's death, had created the vacancy, which John had filled as head teacher of the village school and so he had remained for almost thirty years. John sighed and decided it was time to begin the walk back down to the village.

It was as he walked slowly back down the hill that he had a sort of revelation. Perhaps he had been wrong in his treatment of Amy. Perhaps he had inadvertently caused her death. She had been a lovely girl who had been preyed upon by that young Welshman. Suddenly the horror of what he had done, hit him hard and caused a pain in his chest. Ella too, how could he have been so cruel to her. He must get home and make amends. And little Nan. He must forget the cause of her birth and treat her better. Suddenly it was if clouds had lifted and he was ready to accept his wrongdoing. Was that why his heart was lurching in his chest. Then the pain became excruciating and he fell to the ground.

* * * *

George Atkins was fourteen. His friend Tom Knowles was thirteen and three quarters, as he liked to inform people. But it was the younger boy who instigated most of the mischief they got up to. Soon they would be working on Tomkin's farm. They skived school as much as possible without coming to the attention of old Noble. The school work was no problem as they were both reasonably bright and always ready to help one another out.

That evening, after school, they had been collecting conkers in the churchyard when old Noble went by on his evening walk. Tom suggested they follow him, like Red Indians stalking an enemy and George agreed it would be fun.

They dodged from bush to bush as the headmaster climbed the hill and hid behind a large gorse bush to watch him as he sat on the ground looking down into the valley. He seemed to be day-dreaming. He obviously had no idea he was being spied upon. Sometimes he seemed to be talking to himself and pointing down into the fields. Suddenly he stood up, clasped his chest and stumbled forward a few steps. At that very moment a large fat rabbit popped out of a hole and scrambled between the boys and dashed for the next bush.

'Bloody 'ell, 'said Tom, 'Get a big stick. let's 'ave the bugger. We 'aint 'ad meat at home for weeks.'

George found a stick, but it was too late. The rabbit had gone.

They turned back to Mr Noble, but he couldn't be seen. Then George spotted him. He had fallen forward as if he had tripped over a root or put his foot in a rabbit hole.

'What's up with him' asked Tom.

'Gone to sleep.' said George.

'Reckon he's got any cash in his pockets'

'Worth a look! You done any pick-pocketing.'

'I'll give it a try'

Tom knelt and put his hand in John's pocket. Then stopped and rose abruptly.

'Fucking Hell. He aint asleep. He's fucking dead.'

George gasped then said, 'What do we do?'

'We'll 'ave to tell his missus'

'Will they blame us'

How can they? We say we was just rabbiting, then we found 'im.'

'That sounds all right. So let's get going.'

Chapter 27

Ella had spent a sleepless night worrying about the funeral which was to take place at eleven o'clock that morning. Should she attend or not? After all it was her husband's funeral. But should she go when she had almost hated him for years, since his mistreatment of Amy and her subsequent death. Or should she simply remember the young schoolmaster who had welcomed her and her daughter into his life and given her several years of happiness.

In the end she decided she would not go, whatever the village might think. After all she no longer had any belief in any of that Christian nonsense, since an uncaring God had allowed her daughter to die, and she had not attended the church for many years. The people of the village had accepted her decision, though they did not know the reason. They had always been told that Amy had gone to live abroad.

Having made her decision, Ella made a cup of tea and sat in the kitchen to drink it. Suddenly there was a knock on the door, and when she asked the knocker to come in, she was delighted to see her granddaughter, Nan.

standing there, looking as lively and pretty as ever.

'Nan, Oh Nan. How lovely to see you. You have obviously heard about John.'

'I read about his death in the local paper and that the funeral was today. I came to offer you my support on this sad day.'

'It's so good to see you. I began to think you had left me too.'

'So much has happened. First there was the railway crash just outside Shrewsbury station. I was training to be a nurse and we all had to help the injured. Then I spent while in prison.'

'Prison!'

I was angry. I threw a stone at a window in the Council Offices and it broke. They arrested me and kept me in prison until I had to attend the Magistrates Court. They gave me a warning and a fine but my father, I call him Huw, paid it.'

Ella was amazed. 'You have met your father?'

'Yes, after all these years. He brought me here today. He's waiting outside. He knew that John hated him and wasn't sure about you.'

Oh, bring him in. We've never actually met.'

So Huw entered shyly and Ella knew at once what Amy had seen in him. He was older now but still had a strong upright body, clear cut features and his dark curls were just touched with grey. They shook hands, and Huw whispered, 'Ella, you are so like your daughter I could cry.'

Ella was embarrassed by his compliment and turned to the cooker. 'Would you both like some tea? After all this excitement, I need some more.'

They all sat at the kitchen table to drink their tea. It was Nan who continued the story.

'We went to a town in South Wales to find Huw's sister, the one I am named after. Poor Nan. She had been treated like a servant by her cousin. Now both Nans are going to live with Huw on this farm in the mountains. Huw has bought the farm. He is a rich man.'

'Good heavens, Huw. How did this happen?'

'That's a very long story. Briefly to say it involves finding gold in the Yukon and meeting a man who taught me to invest wisely.'

'Granny, look at the time. You must get dressed if we are to get to the church on time.'

'But I 'm not going.'

'The whole village will be waiting.'

'Very well, but you must stay beside me.'

'Of course I will. What about you Huw?'

'No, this is a family affair. I will take a walk around this village that Amy loved so much.

* * * *

When they left the house, the bell was tolling, its slow, laboured, tone drawing them towards the church. Ella was amazed how many other villagers were walking in the same direction. They did not speak to Ella but nodded sadly and went on. It occurred to Ella that John had taught several generations of the villagers and he had earned their respect, judging him simply as a headmaster, knowing nothing of him as a man. Even the business of John outwitting that wicked rector had been long forgotten.

The church was full when Ella and Nan entered but seats had been kept for them at the front. Ella had not actually met the Rector, even though he had now been here for a number of years, but he seemed to know her. He came straight towards her and shook her hand.

'Mrs Noble. I am the Reverend Oakley. Normally we would have met to discover your wishes for your husband's internment, but I was told that you no longer came to church, so I have devised a service that I thought would be suitable. For instance, I asked the children at school what hymns they sang and which Mr Noble seemed particularly to like. I do hope you find the service appropriate for your husband's life as a headmaster and husband. Perhaps we can meet after the service. In view of your husband's years of public service and his sudden, sad death I shall not be making a charge.'

The Reverend Oakley quickly turned and walked away before Ella had a chance to respond. She watched him signal to the organist and after a brief introduction the first hymn began. As she stood to sing a familiar hymn Ella felt she had never left the church. The whole village seemed to be with her. She already liked Oakley, so different to that Whiting who nearly lost the whole congregation and she knew that John would have loved to sing this hymn.

'Fight the good fight
With all your might'

The service continued smoothly and as Ella looked towards the coffin standing in the aisle, she thought John would have approved.

After the second hymn the vicar gave a short eulogy, describing John's hard work at the school, and his reliability as a church warden and member of the Parish Council. There was mention of the school's success in the annual inspections, and the way his assistants all went on to become qualified teachers. There was no mention of the wife who no longer attended the church, or the daughter who had 'gone abroad' but a brief note was made of the son who was on an expedition to the Antarctic. It was obvious that the young Rector knew as little of John Noble as a person, but his words drew frequent nods from the congregation, as his words fitted their view of their late headmaster.

After the last hymn the Rector gave a short address on the theme of forgiveness. Ella felt her cheeks burning. It was if the Rector knew what she was feeling. She knew that she had hated what John had become these last few years, but should she have forgiven him. She glanced at Nan and remembered the scorn John had poured on their little orphaned granddaughter when Ella insisted, much to John's disgust, that she came to live with them. No, she could not forgive. Ella rose quietly and left the church. No one took much notice; she was obviously overwhelmed.

* * * *

Huw's tour of the village had taken him almost as far as John's last walk. It was pretty village, but without the grandeur of his homeland. When he turned back and had almost reached the church, a man accosted him. He was dressed in the style of a country gentleman and when he spoke it was in an upper-class accent.

'Good morning. I don't believe we have met before. My name is Moreton. Robert Moreton. I am the Squire of Hope Underhill.'

Huw noticed that as he talked the man was observing him closely. It was obvious that his dress, a fine fitted suit in worsted cloth, passed muster.

'My name is Huw Morris. I'm pleased to meet you.'

'A Welsh man I believe'

'Yes indeed.'

'So what is a Welshman doing so far from home.'

Huw wondered if he was being interrogated. But there was no hostility in the man's voice.'

'I brought my daughter to the funeral. You may have met her. She is called Nan.'

'Your daughter? But she lives with the Nobles.'

'She does indeed. Though of course there is only Ella now.'

Robert Moreton looked confused.

'But Nan has lived here most of her life. Yet you say she is your daughter.'

Morton pointed to a nearby bench, and went over to sit on it. He beckoned to Huw to join him. He was obviously intrigued. Huw sat beside him.

'I have been abroad for many years. I did not know that I had a daughter until very recently.'

Moreton paused to consider the matter. 'She is Ella's granddaughter and you are her father. The obvious question is, who is her mother?'

'Her mother is unfortunately dead. Her name was Amy'

'Ah, Amy. You mean Ella's daughter and John's stepdaughter. You say she's dead. But John told me she had gone to live abroad.'

'I suppose that's true. If you believe that Wales is a separate country.'

'Well, this is all news to me. John and I were good friends at one time, but we had drawn apart. I have my responsibilities and he had the school to run. And, I say this in confidence Mr Morris, I felt he was neglecting dear Ella. He had become morose and even bitter. I even thought he had become jealous of my attention to Ella. But she had simply become lonely and appreciated my friendship. That is why I did not attend the funeral. You know how people talk'

'Ah, I heard the church door open. The service must be coming to an end.'

But it was Ella who came out alone, and at the same time a motor car drew up near the churchyard gate. Motor cars were still a rarity in this part of Shropshire. Robert had considered purchasing one, but he still preferred his horses. But the healthy thrum of its internal combustion engine was exciting, and the silence loud when the engine was switched off. A young man got out and hurried to meet Ella. It was her son John.

'Mother.'

'John, but I thought you were far away, sailing to Antarctica.'

Huw and Robert decided that this conversation was not for them so they hurried round the side of the church.

'There has been a problem over supplies. The expedition has been put off till next year. I am staying with a colleague in Shrewsbury. Jack has leant me his car so that I could visit you. So come for a little ride with me. You will enjoy it.'

'Is it safe?'

'Mother, this car is a Rover 20 horsepower. They are built in Coventry. It is one of the best cars you can buy.'

They had reached the car by now and John had helped his mother into her seat. 'So where would you like to go?'

'I have somewhere. But it's rather a long way'

'Look Mother. This car brought me from Shrewsbury in half an hour. It can do forty miles an hour.'

'Very well. Take me to Lake Vyrnwy. I would like to see Amy's grave.'

'Splendid. I have a good road map.'

John checked the controls, then got out of the car and went to the front to crank the starting handle. He had just made the first twist when a voice beside him spoke.

'Hello John. Could you do me an enormous favour?'

Robert raised his hat to Ella, who smiled in return.

'Could I accompany you on this journey. You see I have been considering the purchase of an automobile, and it would give me the opportunity to see how one goes.'

'Mother?'

'That's fine so far as I'm concerned. Huw will look after Nan. So let's get going. I'm quite excited now.'

Robert settled into one of the rear seats. John gave one more turn of the handle and the engine fired. Then they were off, with Huw waving them forward and the congregation, who were just leaving the church, commenting loudly on the scene before them.

* * * *

There wasn't much conversation on the journey because the sound of engine and the wind created by their passage made hearing difficult, Young John told them about Amy.

'My half-sister was much older than me. She was a young woman while I was still a child. But she was always kind and very pretty.'

Ella nodded.

Some while later John asked his mother, 'How did the old man's funeral go? His mother answered simply. 'Your father would have liked it.' John, who was still angry with his father said no more.

The road beyond Llanfyllin was less well made. The car coped well, but frequent pot holes caused Robert to bounce off his seat with great hilarity and cries of 'Steady the buffs!' Soon they were on top of the hills where no one seemed to live and only sheep filled the fields. At last they began to descend towards the lake. Just before they reached the water Ella lifted her head from the map she had been perusing and told John to stop, saying, 'We must walk the rest of the way.'

John drew in to a parking place. On the opposite side of the road a narrow lane rose steeply and a sign announced, 'St Wddyn's Church'. Memories of that sad occasion, when she had buried her daughter came to Ella and her eyes filled with tears. Robert took her arm as they crossed the road and began walking up the lane.

'Huw told me of Amy's death. But why is she buried here?'

'Because John would not allow her body to be brought back to Hope Underhill. He did not want the villagers to know that she had died.'

They climbed the steep lane until at last they reached the little church which had been built to replace the one now deep under the water of the lake. Robert stood looking at the scene and exclaimed, 'Well Amy has a wonderful resting place.'

Ella smiled in agreement.

John said, 'I know that she was forced to live a life she didn't want for the sake of little Nan, but she was a good woman who didn't deserve to die.'

'We must remember her the way we knew her' added Robert.

Ella led them to the grave, and sank to her knees in the wet grass. She had had a simple gravestone erected without her husband's knowledge. The inscription read 'Beloved Amy. Taken too soon.'

Ella's tears flowed once more. Robert took her hand and lifted her up, holding on for rather longer than was perhaps necessary.

Ella did not remove his hand, but bent forward to brush the dirt from her skirt, hide her blushes and smile at the thought of a happier life to come.

The End

Printed in Great Britain
by Amazon

61767440R00133